PENGUIN BOOKS

FOR YOUR EYES ONLY

Ian Fleming was born in 1908 and educated at Eton. After a brief period at the Royal Military Academy at Sandhurst he went abroad to further his education. In 1931, having failed to get an appointment in the Foreign Office, he joined Reuters News Agency. During the Second World War he was Personal Assistant to the Director of Naval Intelligence at the Admiralty, rising to the rank of Commander. His wartime experiences provided him with a first-hand knowledge of secret operations.

After the war he became Foreign Manager of Kemsley Newspapers. He built his house, Goldeneye, in Jamaica and there at the age of forty-four he wrote *Casino Royale,* the first of the novels featuring Commander James Bond. By the time of his death in 1964, the James Bond adventures had sold more than forty million copies. *Doctor No,* the first film featuring James Bond and starring Sean Connery, was released in 1962 and the Bond films continue to be huge international successes. He is also the author of the magical children's book *Chitty Chitty Bang Bang.*

The novels of Ian Fleming were immediately recognized as classic thrillers by his contemporaries Kingsley Amis, Raymond Chandler and John Betjeman. With the invention of James Bond, Ian Fleming created the greatest British fictional icon of the late twentieth century.

For more information about Ian Fleming's life and works, please visit the official Web site of Ian Fleming Publications Ltd: www.ianflemingcentre.com

FOR YOUR EYES ONLY

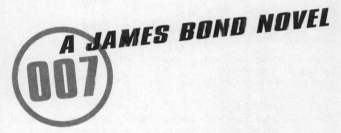

A JAMES BOND NOVEL

007

BY **IAN FLEMING**

PENGUIN BOOKS

PENGUIN BOOKS
Published by the Penguin Group
Penguin Group (USA) Inc., 375 Hudson Street,
New York, New York 10014, U.S.A.
Penguin Books Ltd, 80 Strand,
London WC2R 0RL, England
Penguin Books Australia Ltd, 250 Camberwell Road,
Camberwell, Victoria 3124, Australia
Penguin Books Canada Ltd, 10 Alcorn Avenue,
Toronto, Ontario, Canada M4V 3B2
Penguin Books India (P) Ltd, 11 Community Centre,
Panchsheel Park, New Delhi-110 017, India
Penguin Books (N.Z.) Ltd, Cnr Rosedale and Airborne Roads,
Albany, Auckland, New Zealand
Penguin Books (South Africa) (Pty) Ltd, 24 Sturdee Avenue,
Rosebank, Johannesburg 2196, South Africa

Penguin Books Ltd, Registered Offices:
80 Strand, London, WC2R 0RL, England

First published in Great Britain by Jonathan Cape Ltd. 1960
First published in the United States of America by The Viking Press 1960
Published in Penguin Books (U.K.) 2002
Published in Penguin Books (U.S.A.) 2003

10 9 8

LIBRARY OF CONGRESS CATALOGING IN PUBLICATION DATA
Fleming, Ian, 1908–1964.
  For your eyes only / Ian Fleming.
    p. cm.
  ISBN 0 14 20.0322 0
    1. Bond, James (Fictitious character)—Fiction.   2. British—Foreign countries—
Fiction.   3. Intelligence officers—Fiction.   4. Spy stories, English.   I. Title.
  PR6056.L4F6 2003
  823'.914—dc21   2003040486

Printed in the United States of America
Set in Melior

CONTENTS

The eyes behind the wide black rubber goggles were cold as flint. In the howling speed-turmoil of a BSA M20 doing seventy, they were the only quiet things in the hurtling flesh and metal. Protected by the glass of the goggles, they stared fixedly ahead from just above the centre of the handlebars, and their dark unwavering focus was that of gun muzzles. Below the goggles, the wind had got into the face through the mouth and had wrenched the lips back into a square grin that showed big tombstone teeth and strips of whitish gum. On both sides of the grin the cheeks had been blown out by the wind into pouches that fluttered slightly. To right and left of the hurtling face under the crash helmet, the black gauntlets, broken-wristed at the controls, looked like the attacking paws of a big animal.

The man was dressed in the uniform of a dispatch-rider in the Royal Corps of Signals, and his machine, painted olive green, was, with certain modifications to the valves and the carburettor and the removal of some of the silencer baffles to give more speed, identical with a standard British Army machine. There was nothing in the man or his equipment to suggest that he was not what he appeared to be, except a fully loaded Luger held by a clip to the top of the petrol tank.

It was seven o'clock on a May morning and the dead straight road through the forest glittered with the tiny luminous mist of spring. On both sides of the road the moss- and flower-carpeted depths between the great oak trees held the theatrical enchantment of the royal forests of Versailles and St Germain. The road was D98, a secondary road serving local traffic in the St Germain area, and the motor-cyclist had just passed beneath the Paris-Mantes autoroute already thundering with commuter traffic for Paris. He was heading north towards St Germain and there was no one else in sight in either direction, except, perhaps half a mile ahead, an almost identical figure—another Royal Corps dispatch-rider. He was a younger, slimmer man and he sat comfortably back on his machine, enjoying the morning and keeping his speed to around forty. He was well on time and it was a beautiful day. He wondered whether to have his eggs fried or scrambled when he got back to HQ around eight.

Five hundred yards, four hundred, three, two, one. The man coming up from behind slowed to fifty. He put his right gauntlet up to his teeth and pulled it off. He stuffed the gauntlet between the buttons of his tunic and reached down and unclipped the gun.

By now he must have been big in the driving-mirror of the young man ahead, for suddenly the young man jerked his head round, surprised to find another dispatch-rider on his run at that time of the morning. He expected that it would be an American or perhaps French military police. It might be anyone from the eight NATO nations that made up the staff of SHAPE, but when he recognized the uniform of the Corps he was astonished and delighted. Who the hell could it be? He raised a cheerful right thumb in recognition and cut his speed to thirty, waiting for the other man to drift up alongside. With one eye on the road ahead and the other on the approaching silhouette in the mirror, he ran through the names of the British riders in the Special Service Transportation Unit at Headquarters Command. Albert, Sid, Wally—might be Wally, same thick build. Good show! He'd be able to pull his leg about that little frog bit in the canteen—Louise, Elise, Lise— what the hell was her name.

The man with the gun had slowed. Now he was fifty yards away. His face, undistorted by the wind, had set into blunt, hard, perhaps Slav lines. A red spark burned behind the black, aimed muzzles of the eyes. Forty yards, thirty. A single magpie flew out of the forest ahead of the young dispatch-rider. It fled clumsily across the road into the bushes behind a Michelin sign that said that St Germain was one kilometre to go. The young man grinned and raised an ironical finger in salute and self-protection—'One magpie is sorrow'.

Twenty yards behind him the man with the gun took both hands off the handlebars, lifted the Luger, rested it carefully on his left forearm and fired one shot.

The young man's hands whipped off his controls and met across the centre of his backward-arching spine. His machine veered across the road, jumped a narrow ditch and ploughed into a patch of grass and lilies of the valley. There it rose up on its screaming back wheel and slowly crashed backwards on top of its dead rider. The BSA coughed and kicked and tore at the young man's clothes and at the flowers, and then lay quiet.

The killer executed a narrow turn and stopped with his machine pointing back the way he had come. He stamped down the wheel-rest, pulled his machine up on to it and walked in among the wild flowers under the trees. He knelt down beside the dead man and brusquely pulled back an eyelid. Just as roughly he tore the black leather dispatch-case off the corpse and ripped open the buttons of the tunic and removed a battered leather wallet. He wrenched a cheap wristwatch so sharply off the left wrist that the chrome expanding bracelet snapped in half. He stood up and slung the dispatch-case over his shoulder. While he stowed the wallet and the watch away in his tunic pocket he listened. There were only forest sounds and the slow tick of hot metal from the crashed BSA. The killer retraced his steps to the road. He walked slowly, scuffing leaves over the tyre marks in the soft earth and moss. He took extra trouble over the deep scars in the ditch and the grass verge, and then stood beside his motor-cycle and looked back towards the lily of the valley patch. Not bad! Probably only the police dogs would get it, and, with ten miles of road to cover, they would be hours, perhaps days—plenty long enough. The main thing in these jobs was to have enough safety margin. He could have shot the man at forty yards, but he had preferred to get to twenty. And taking the watch and the wallet had been nice touches—pro touches.

Pleased with himself, the man heaved his machine off its rest, vaulted smartly into the saddle and kicked down on the starter. Slowly, so as not to show skid marks, he accelerated away back down the road and in a minute or so he was doing seventy again and the wind had redrawn the empty turnip grin across his face.

Around the scene of the killing, the forest, which had held its breath while it was done, slowly began to breathe again.

James Bond had his first drink of the evening at Fouquet's. It was not a solid drink. One cannot drink seriously in French cafés. Out of doors on a pavement in the sun is no place for vodka or whisky or gin. A *fine à l'eau* is fairly serious, but it intoxicates without tasting very good. A *quart de champagne* or a *champagne à l'orange* is all right before luncheon, but in the evening one *quart* leads to another *quart* and a bottle of indifferent champagne is a bad foundation for the night. Pernod is possible, but it should be drunk in company, and anyway Bond had never liked the stuff because its liquorice taste reminded him of his childhood. No, in cafés you have to drink the least offensive of the musical comedy drinks that go with them, and Bond always had the same thing—an Americano—Bitter Campari, Cinzano, a large slice of lemon peel and soda. For the soda he always stipulated Perrier, for in his opinion expensive soda water was the cheapest way to improve a poor drink.

When Bond was in Paris he invariably stuck to the same addresses. He stayed at the Terminus Nord, because he liked station hotels and because this was the least pretentious and most anonymous of them. He had luncheon at the Café de la Paix, the Rotonde or the Dôme, because the food was good enough and it amused him to watch the people. If he wanted a solid drink he had it at Harry's Bar, both because of the solidity of the drinks and because, on his first ignorant visit to Paris at the age of sixteen, he had done what Harry's advertisement in the *Continental Daily Mail* had told him to do and had said to his taxi-driver 'Sank Roo Doe Noo'. That had started one of the memorable evenings of his life, culminating in the loss, almost simultaneous, of his virginity and his notecase. For dinner, Bond went to one of the great restaurants—Véfour, the Caneton, Lucas-Carton or the Cochon d'Or. These he considered, whatever Michelin might say about the Tour d'Argent, Maxims and the like, to have somehow avoided the tarnish of the expense account and the dollar. Anyway, he preferred their cooking. After dinner he generally went to the Place Pigalle to see what would happen to him. When, as usual, nothing did, he would walk home across Paris to the Gare du Nord and go to bed.

Tonight Bond decided to tear up this dusty address-book and have himself an old-fashioned ball. He was on his way through Paris after a dismally failed assignment on the Austro-Hungarian border. It had been a question of getting a certain Hungarian out. Bond had been sent from London specially to direct the operation over the head of Station V. This had been unpopular with the Vienna Station. There had been misunderstandings—wilful ones. The man had been killed in the frontier minefield. There would have to be a court of inquiry. Bond was due back at his London headquarters on the following day to make his report, and the thought of it all depressed him. Today had been so beautiful—one of those days when you almost believe that Paris is beautiful and gay—and Bond had decided to give the town just one more chance. He would somehow find himself a girl who was a real girl, and he would take her to dinner at some make-believe place in the Bois like the Armenonville. To clean the money-look out of her eyes—for it would certainly be there—he would as soon as possible give her fifty thousand francs. He would say to her: 'I propose to call you Donatienne, or possibly Solange, because these are names that suit my mood and the evening. We knew each other before and you lent me this money because I was in a jam. Here it is, and now we will tell each other what we have been doing since we last met in St Tropez just a year ago. In the meantime, here is the menu and the wine list and you must choose what will make you happy and fat.' And she would look relieved at not having to try any more, and she would laugh and say: 'But, James, I do not want to be fat.' And there they would be, started on the myth of 'Paris in the Spring', and Bond would stay sober and be interested in her and everything she said. And, by God, by the end of the evening it would not be his fault if it transpired that there was in fact no shred of stuffing left in the hoary old fairytale of 'A good time in Paris'.

Sitting in Fouquet's, waiting for his Americano, Bond smiled at his vehemence. He knew that he was only playing at this fantasy for the satisfaction of launching a last kick at a town he had cordially disliked since the War. Since 1945, he had not had a happy day in Paris. It was not that the town had sold its body. Many towns have done that. It was its heart that

was gone—pawned to the tourists, pawned to the Russians
and Roumanians and Bulgars, pawned to the scum of the
world who had gradually taken the town over. And, of course,
pawned to the Germans. You could see it in the people's
eyes—sullen, envious, ashamed. Architecture? Bond glanced
across the pavement at the shiny black ribbons of cars off
which the sun glinted painfully. Everywhere it was the same
as in the Champs-Elysées. There were only two hours in
which you could even see the town—between five and seven
in the morning. After seven it was engulfed in a thundering
stream of black metal with which no beautiful buildings, no
spacious, tree-lined boulevards, could compete.

The waiter's tray clattered down on the marble-topped
table. With a slick one-handed jerk that Bond had never been
able to copy, the waiter's bottle-opener prised the cap off the
Perrier. The man slipped the tab under the ice-bucket, said a
mechanical 'Voilà, M'sieur' and darted away. Bond put ice
into his drink, filled it to the top with soda and took a long
pull at it. He sat back and lit a Laurens jaune. Of course the
evening would be a disaster. Even supposing he found the girl
in the next hour or so, the contents would certainly not stand
up to the wrapping. On closer examination she would turn
out to have the heavy, dank, wide-pored skin of the bourgeois
French. The blonde hair under the rakish velvet beret would
be brown at the roots and as coarse as piano wire. The pepper-
mint on the breath would not conceal the midday garlic. The
alluring figure would be intricately scaffolded with wire and
rubber. She would be from Lille and she would ask him if he
was American. And, Bond smiled to himself, she or her *ma-
quereau* would probably steal his notecase. La ronde! He
would be back where he came in. More or less, that was. Well,
to hell with it!

A battered black Peugeot 403 broke out of the centre stream
of traffic, cut across the inside line of cars and pulled in to

double park at the kerb. There was the usual screaming of brakes, hooting and yelling. Quite unmoved, a girl got out of the car and, leaving the traffic to sort itself out, walked purposefully across the sidewalk. Bond sat up. She had everything, but absolutely everything that belonged in his fantasy. She was tall and, although her figure was hidden by a light raincoat, the way she moved and the way she held herself promised that it would be beautiful. The face had the gaiety and bravado that went with her driving, but now there was impatience in the compressed lips and the eyes fretted as she pushed diagonally through the moving crowd on the pavement.

Bond watched her narrowly as she reached the edge of the tables and came up the aisle. Of course it was hopeless. She was coming to meet someone—her lover. She was the sort of woman who always belongs to somebody else. She was late for him. That's why she was in such a hurry. What damnable luck—right down to the long blonde hair under the rakish beret! And she was looking straight at him. She was smiling . . . !

Before Bond could pull himself together, the girl had come up to his table and had drawn out a chair and sat down.

She smiled rather tautly into his startled eyes. 'I'm sorry I'm late, and I'm afraid we've got to get moving at once. You're wanted at the office.' She added under her breath: 'Crash dive.'

Bond jerked himself back to reality. Whoever she was, she was certainly from 'the firm'. 'Crash dive' was a slang expression the Secret Service had borrowed from the Submarine Service. It meant bad news—the worst. Bond dug into his pocket and slid some coins over the table. He said 'Right. Let's go,' and got up and followed her down through the tables and across to her car. It was still obstructing the inner lane of traffic. Any minute now there would be a policeman. Angry faces glared at them as they climbed in. The girl had left the engine running. She banged the gears into second and slid out into the traffic.

Bond looked sideways at her. The pale skin was velvet. The blonde hair was silk—to the roots. He said: 'Where are you from and what's it all about?'

She said, concentrating on the traffic: 'From the Station. Grade two assistant. Number 765 on duty, Mary Ann Russell off. I've no idea what it's all about. I just saw the signal from HQ—personal from M to Head of Station. Most Immediate and all that. He was to find you at once and if necessary use the Deuxième to help. Head of F said you always went to the same places when you were in Paris, and I and another girl were given a list.' She smiled. 'I'd only tried Harry's Bar, and after Fouquet's I was going to start on the restaurants. It was marvellous picking you up like that.' She gave him a quick glance. 'I hope I wasn't very clumsy.'

Bond said: 'You were fine. How were you going to handle it if I'd had a girl with me?'

She laughed. 'I was going to do much the same except call you "sir". I was only worried about how you'd dispose of the girl. If she started a scene I was going to offer to take her home in my car and for you to take a taxi.'

'You sound pretty resourceful. How long have you been in the Service?'

'Five years. This is my first time with a Station.'

'How do you like it?'

'I like the work all right. The evenings and days off drag a bit. It's not easy to make friends in Paris without'—her mouth turned down with irony—'without all the rest. I mean,' she hastened to add, 'I'm not a prude and all that, but somehow the French make the whole business such a bore. I mean I've had to give up taking the Metro or buses. Whatever time of day it is, you end up with your behind black and blue.' She laughed. 'Apart from the boredom of it and not knowing what to say to the man, some of the pinches really hurt. It's the limit. So to get around I bought this car cheap, and other cars seem to keep out of my way. As long as you don't catch the other driver's eye, you can take on even the meanest of them. They're afraid you haven't seen them. And they're worried by the bashed-about look of the car. They give you a wide berth.'

They had come to the Rond Point. As if to demonstrate her theory, she tore round it and went straight at the line of traffic coming up from the Place de la Concorde. Miraculously it divided and let her through into the Avenue Matignon.

Bond said: 'Pretty good. But don't make it a habit. There may be some French Mary Anns about.'

She laughed. She turned into the Avenue Gabrielle and pulled up outside the Paris headquarters of the Secret Service: 'I only try that sort of manœuvre in the line of duty.'

Bond got out and came round to her side of the car. He said: 'Well, thanks for picking me up. When this whirl is over, can I pick you up in exchange? I don't get the pinches, but I'm just as bored in Paris as you are.'

Her eyes were blue and wide apart. They searched his. She said seriously: 'I'd like that. The switchboard here can always find me.'

Bond reached in through the window and pressed the hand on the wheel. He said 'Good,' and turned and walked quickly in through the archway.

Wing Commander Rattray, Head of Station F, was a fattish man with pink cheeks and fair hair brushed straight back. He dressed in a mannered fashion with turned-back cuffs and double slits to his coat, bow-ties and fancy waistcoats. He made a good-living, wine-and-food-society impression in which only the slow, rather cunning blue eyes struck a false note. He chain-smoked Gauloises and his office stank of them. He greeted Bond with relief. 'Who found you?'

'Russell. At Fouquet's. Is she new?'

'Six months. She's a good one. But take a pew. There's the hell of a flap on and I've got to brief you and get you going.' He bent to his intercom and pressed down a switch. 'Signal to M, please. Personal from Head of Station. "Located 007 briefing now." Okay?' He let go the switch.

Bond pulled a chair over by the open window to keep away from the fog of Gauloises. The traffic on the Champs-Elysées was a soft roar in the background. Half an hour before he had been fed up with Paris, glad to be going. Now he hoped he would be staying.

Head of F said: 'Somebody got our dawn dispatch-rider from SHAPE to the St Germain Station yesterday morning. The weekly run from the SHAPE Intelligence Division with the Summaries, Joint Intelligence papers, Iron Curtain Order of Battle—all the top gen. One shot in the back. Took his dispatch-case and his wallet and watch.'

Bond said: 'That's bad. No chance that it was an ordinary hold-up? Or do they think the wallet and watch were cover?'

'SHAPE Security can't make up their minds. On the whole they guess it was cover. Seven o'clock in the morning's a rum time for a hold-up. But you can argue it out with them when you get down there. M's sending you as his personal representative. He's worried as hell. Apart from the loss of the Intelligence dope, their I. people have never liked having one of our Stations outside the Reservation so to speak. For years they've been trying to get the St Germain unit incorporated in the SHAPE Intelligence set-up. But you know what M is, independent old devil. He's never been happy about NATO Security. Why, right in the SHAPE Intelligence Division there are not only a couple of Frenchmen and an Italian, but the head of their Counter Intelligence and Security section is a German!'

Bond whistled.

'The trouble is that this damnable business is all SHAPE needs to bring M to heel. Anyway, he says you're to get down there right away. I've fixed up clearance for you. Got the passes. You're to report to Colonel Schreiber, Headquarters Command Security Branch. American. Efficient chap. He's been handling the thing from the beginning. As far as I can gather, he's already done just about all there was to be done.'

'What's he done? What actually happened?'

Head of F picked up a map from his desk and walked over with it. It was the big-scale Michelin *Environs de Paris*. He pointed with a pencil. 'Here's Versailles, and here, just north of the park, is the big junction of the Paris-Mantes and the Versailles autoroutes. A couple of hundred yards north of that, on N184, is SHAPE. Every Wednesday, at seven in the morning, a Special Services dispatch-rider leaves SHAPE with the weekly Intelligence stuff I told you about. He has to get to this little village called Fourqueux, just outside St Germain, deliver his stuff to the duty officer at our HQ, and report back to SHAPE by seven-thirty. Rather than go through all this built-up area, for security reasons his orders are to take this N307 to St Nom, turn right-handed on to D98 and go under the autoroute and through the forest of St Germain. The distance is about twelve kilometres, and taking it easy he'll do the trip in under a quarter of an hour. Well, yesterday it was a corporal from the Corps of Signals, good solid man called Bates, and when he hadn't reported back to SHAPE by seven-forty-five they sent another rider to look for him. Not a trace, and he hadn't reported at our HQ. By eight-fifteen the Security Branch was on the job, and by nine the roadblocks were up. The police and the Deuxième were told and search parties got under way. The dogs found him, but not till the evening around six, and by that time if there had been any clues on the road they'd have been wiped out by the traffic.' Head of F handed the map to Bond and walked back to his desk. 'And that's about the lot, except that all the usual steps have been taken—frontiers, ports, aerodromes and so forth. But that sort of thing won't help. If it was a professional job, whoever did it could have had the stuff out of the country by midday or into an embassy in Paris inside an hour.'

Bond said impatiently: 'Exactly! And so what the hell does M expect me to do? Tell SHAPE Security to do it all over again, but better? This sort of thing isn't my line at all. Bloody waste of time.'

Head of F smiled sympathetically. 'Matter of fact I put much the same point of view to M over the scrambler. Tactfully. The old man was quite reasonable. Said he wanted to show SHAPE he was taking the business just as seriously as they were. You happened to be available and more or less on the spot, and he said you had the sort of mind that might pick up the invisible factor. I asked him what he meant, and he said that at all closely guarded headquarters there's bound to be an invisible man—a man everyone takes so much for granted that he just isn't noticed—gardener, window cleaner, postman. I said that SHAPE had thought of that, and that all those sort of jobs were done by enlisted men. M told me not to be so literal-minded and hung up.'

Bond laughed. He could see M's frown and hear the crusty voice. He said: 'All right, then. I'll see what I can do. Who do I report back to?'

'Here. M doesn't want the St Germain unit to get involved. Anything you have to say I'll put straight on the printer to London. But I may not be available when you call up. I'll make someone your duty officer and you'll be able to get them any time in the twenty-four hours. Russell can do it. She picked you up. She might as well carry you. Suit you?'

'Yes,' said Bond. 'That'll be all right.'

The battered Peugeot, commandeered by Rattray, smelled of her. There were bits of her in the glove compartment—half a packet of Suchard milk chocolate, a twist of paper containing bobby pins, a paperback John O'Hara, a single black suede glove. Bond thought about her as far as the Etoile and then closed his mind to her and pushed the car along fast through the Bois. Rattray had said it would take about fifteen minutes at fifty. Bond said to halve the speed and double the time and to tell Colonel Schreiber that he would be with him by nine-thirty. After the Porte de St Cloud there was little traffic, and Bond held seventy on the autoroute until the second exit road came up on his right and there was the red arrow for SHAPE. Bond turned up the slope and on to N184. Two hundred yards farther, in the centre of the road, was the traffic policeman Bond had been told to look out for. The policeman waved him in through the big gates on the left and he pulled up at the first checkpoint. A grey-uniformed American policeman hung out of his cabin and glanced at his pass. He was told to pull inside and hold it. Now a French policeman took his pass, noted the details on a printed form clipped to a board, gave him a large plastic windscreen number and waved him on. As Bond pulled in to the car park, with theatrical suddenness a hundred arc-lights blazed and lit up the acre of low-lying hutments in front of him as if it was day. Feeling naked, Bond walked across the open gravel beneath the flags of the NATO countries and ran up the four shallow steps to the wide glass doors that gave entrance to the Supreme Headquarters Allied Forces Europe. Now there was the main Security desk. American and French military police checked his pass and noted the details. He was handed over to a red-capped British MP and led off down the main corridor past endless office doors. They bore no names but the usual alphabetical abracadabra of all headquarters. One said COMSTRIKFLTLANT AND SACLANT LIAISON TO SACEUR. Bond asked what it meant. The military policeman, either ignorant or, more probably, security-minded, said stolidly: 'Couldn't rightly say, sir.'

Behind a door that said *Colonel G. A. Schreiber, Chief of Security, Headquarters Command*, was a ramrod-straight, middle-aged American with greying hair and the politely negative manner of a bank manager. There were several family photographs in silver frames on his desk and a vase containing one white rose. There was no smell of tobacco smoke in the room. After cautiously amiable preliminaries, Bond congratulated the Colonel on his security. He said: 'All these checks and double checks don't make it easy for the opposition. Have you ever lost anything before, or have you ever found signs of a serious attempt at a coup?'

'No to both questions, Commander. I'm quite satisfied about Headquarters. It's only the outlying units that worry me. Apart from this section of your Secret Service, we have various detached signal units. Then, of course, there are the Home Ministries of fourteen different nations. I can't answer for what may leak from those quarters.'

'It can't be an easy job,' agreed Bond. 'Now, about this mess. Has anything else come up since Wing Commander Rattray spoke to you last?'

'Got the bullet. Luger. Severed the spinal cord. Probably fired at around thirty yards, give or take ten yards. Assuming our man was riding a straight course, the bullet must have been fired from dead astern on a level trajectory. Since it can't have been a man standing in the road, the killer must have been moving in or on some vehicle.'

'So your man would have seen him in the driving-mirror?'

'Probably.'

'If your riders find themselves being followed, do they have any instructions about taking evasive action?'

The Colonel smiled slightly. 'Sure. They're told to go like hell.'

'And at what speed did your man crash?'

'Not fast, they think. Between twenty and forty. What are you getting at, Commander?'

'I was wondering if you'd decided whether it was a pro or an amateur job. If your man wasn't trying to get away, and assuming he saw the killer in his mirror, which I agree is only a probability, that suggests that he accepted the man on his tail as friend rather than foe. That could mean some sort of disguise that would fit in with the set-up here—something your man would accept even at that hour of the morning.'

A small frown had been gathering across Colonel Schreiber's smooth forehead. 'Commander,' there was an edge of tension in the voice, 'we have, of course, been considering every angle of this case, including the one you mention. At midday yesterday the Commanding General declared emergency in this matter, standing security and security ops committees were set up, and from that moment on every angle, every hint of a clue, has been systematically run to earth. And I can tell you, Commander,' the Colonel raised one well-manicured hand and let it descend in soft emphasis on his blotting-pad, 'any man who can come up with an even remotely original idea on this case will have to be closely related to Einstein. There is nothing, repeat nothing, to go on in this case whatsoever.'

Bond smiled sympathetically. He got to his feet. 'In that case, Colonel, I won't waste any more of your time this evening. If I could just have the minutes of the various meetings to bring myself up to date, and if one of your men could show me the way to the canteen and my quarters . . .'

'Sure, sure.' The Colonel pressed a bell. A young crew-cutted aide came in. 'Proctor, show the Commander to his room in the VIP wing, would you, and then take him along to the bar and the canteen.' He turned to Bond. 'I'll have those papers ready for you after you've had a meal and a drink. They'll be in my office. They can't be taken out, of course, but you'll find everything to hand next door, and Proctor will be able to fill you in on anything that's missing.' He held out his hand. 'Okay? Then we'll meet again in the morning.'

Bond said goodnight and followed the aide out. As he walked along the neutral-painted, neutral-smelling corridors, he reflected that this was probably the most hopeless assignment he had ever been on. If the top security brains of fourteen countries were stumped, what hope had he got? By the time he was in bed that night, in the Spartan luxury of the visitors' overnight quarters, Bond had decided he would give it a couple more days—largely for the sake of keeping in touch with Mary Ann Russell for as long as possible—and then chuck it. On this decision he fell immediately into a deep and untroubled sleep.

Not two, but four days later, as the dawn came up over the Forest of St Germain, James Bond was lying along the thick branch of an oak tree keeping watch over a small empty glade that lay deep among the trees bordering D98, the road of the murder.

He was dressed from head to foot in parachutists' camouflage—green, brown and black. Even his hands were covered with the stuff, and there was a hood over his head with slits cut for the eyes and mouth. It was good camouflage which would be still better when the sun was higher and the shadows blacker, and from anywhere on the ground, even directly below the high branch, he could not be seen.

It had come about like this. The first two days at SHAPE had been the expected waste of time. Bond had achieved nothing except to make himself mildly unpopular with the persistence of his double-checking questions. On the morning of the third day he was about to go and say his goodbyes when he had a telephone call from the Colonel. 'Oh, Commander, thought I'd let you know that the last team of police dogs got in late last night—your idea that it might be worth while covering the whole forest. Sorry'—the voice sounded un-sorry—'but negative, absolutely negative.'

'Oh. My fault for the wasted time.' As much to annoy the Colonel as anything, Bond said: 'Mind if I have a talk with the handler?'

'Sure, sure. Anything you want. By the way, Commander, how long are you planning to be around? Glad to have you with us for as long as you like. But it's a question of your room. Seems there's a big party coming in from Holland in a few days' time. Top level staff course or something of the kind, and Admin says they're a bit pushed for space.'

Bond had not expected to get on well with Colonel Schreiber and he had not done so. He said amiably: 'I'll see what my Chief has to say and call you back, Colonel.'

'Do that, would you.' The Colonel's voice was equally polite, but the manners of both men were running out and the two receivers broke the line simultaneously.

The chief handler was a Frenchman from the Landes. He had the quick sly eyes of a poacher. Bond met him at the kennels, but the handler's proximity was too much for the Alsatians and, to get away from the noise, he took Bond into the duty-room, a tiny office with binoculars hanging from pegs, and waterproofs, gumboots, dog-harness and other gear stacked round the walls. There were a couple of deal chairs and a table covered with a large-scale map of the Forest of St Germain. This had been marked off into pencilled squares. The handler made a gesture over the map. 'Our dogs covered it all, Monsieur. There is nothing there.'

'Do you mean to say they didn't check once?'

The handler scratched his head. 'We had trouble with a bit

of game, Monsieur. There was a hare or two. A couple of foxes' earths. We had quite a time getting them away from a clearing near the Carrefour Royal. They probably still smelled the gipsies.'

'Oh.' Bond was only mildly interested 'Show me. Who were these gipsies?'

The handler pointed daintily with a grimy little finger. 'These are the names from the old days. Here is the Etoile Parfaite, and here, where the killing took place, is the Carrefour des Curieux. And here, forming the bottom of the triangle, is the Carrefour Royal. It makes,' he added dramatically, 'a cross with the road of death.' He took a pencil out of his pocket and made a dot just off the crossroads. 'And this is the clearing, Monsieur. There was a gipsy caravan there for most of the winter. They left last month. Cleaned the place up all right, but, for the dogs, their scent will hang about there for months.'

Bond thanked him, and after inspecting and admiring the dogs and making some small talk about the handler's profession, he got into the Peugeot and went off to the gendarmerie in St Germain. 'Yes, certainly they had known the gipsies. Real Romany-looking fellows. Hardly spoke a word of French, but they had behaved themselves. There had been no complaints. Six men and two women. No. No one had seen them go. One morning they just weren't there any more. Might have been gone a week for all one knew. They had chosen an isolated spot.'

Bond took the D98 through the forest. When the great autoroute bridge showed up a quarter of a mile ahead over the road, Bond accelerated and then switched off the engine and coasted silently until he came to the Carrefour Royal. He stopped and got out of the car without a sound, and, feeling rather foolish, softly entered the forest and walked with great circumspection towards where the clearing would be. Twenty yards inside the trees he came to it. He stood in the fringe of bushes and trees and examined it carefully. Then he walked in and went over it from end to end.

The clearing was about as big as two tennis courts and floored in thick grass and moss. There was one large patch of lilies of the valley and, under the bordering trees, a scattering of bluebells. To one side there was a low mound, perhaps a tumulus, completely surrounded and covered with brambles and brier roses now thickly in bloom. Bond walked round this and gazed in among the roots, but there was nothing to see except the earthy shape of the mound.

Bond took one last look round and then went to the corner of the clearing that would be nearest to the road. Here there was easy access through the trees. Were there traces of a path, a slight flattening of the leaves? Not more than would have been left by the gipsies or last year's picnickers. On the edge of the road there was a narrow passage between two trees. Casually Bond bent to examine the trunks. He stiffened and dropped to a crouch. With a fingernail, he delicately scraped away a narrow sliver of caked mud. It hid a deep scratch in the tree-trunk. He caught the scraps of mud in his free hand. He now spat and moistened the mud and carefully filled up the scratch again. There were three camouflaged scratches on one tree and four on the other. Bond walked quickly out of the trees on to the road. His car had stopped on a slight slope leading down under the autoroute bridge. Although there was some protection from the boom of the traffic on the autoroute, Bond pushed the car, jumped in and only engaged the gears when he was well under the bridge.

And now Bond was back in the clearing, above it, and he still did not know if his hunch had been right. It had been M's dictum that had put him on the scent—if it was a scent—and the mention of the gipsies. 'It was the gipsies the dogs smelled . . . Most of the winter . . . they went last month. No complaints . . . One morning they just weren't there any

more.' The invisible factor. The invisible man. The people
who are so much part of the background that you don't know
if they're there or not. Six men and two girls and they hardly
spoke a word of French. Good cover, gipsies. You could be a
foreigner and yet not a foreigner, because you were only a
gipsy. Some of them had gone off in the caravan. Had some of
them stayed, built themselves a hide-out during the winter, a
secret place from which the hijacking of the top secret dis-
patches had been the first sortie? Bond had thought he was
building fantasies until he found the scratches, the carefully
camouflaged scratches, on the two trees. They were just at the
height where, if one was carrying any kind of a cycle, the ped-
als might catch against the bark. It could all be a pipedream,
but it was good enough for Bond. The only question in his
mind was whether these people had made a one-time-only
coup or whether they were so confident of their security that
they would try again. He confided only in Station F. Mary
Ann Russell told him to be careful. Head of F, more construc-
tively, ordered his unit at St Germain to cooperate. Bond said
goodbye to Colonel Schreiber and moved to a camp bed in the
unit's HQ—an anonymous house in an anonymous village
back street. The unit had provided the camouflage outfit and
the four Secret Service men who ran the unit had happily put
themselves under Bond's orders. They realized as well as
Bond did that if Bond managed to wipe the eye of the whole
security machine of SHAPE, the Secret Service would have
won a priceless feather in its cap *vis-à-vis* the SHAPE High
Command, and M's worries over the independence of his unit
would be gone for ever.

Bond, lying along the oak branch, smiled to himself. Private
armies, private wars. How much energy they siphoned off
from the common cause, how much fire they directed away
from the common enemy!

Six-thirty. Time for breakfast. Cautiously Bond's right hand fumbled in his clothing and came up to the slit of his mouth. Bond made the glucose tablet last as long as possible and then sucked another. His eyes never left the glade. The red squirrel that had appeared at first light and had been steadily eating away at young beech shoots ever since, ran a few feet nearer to the rose-bushes on the mound, picked up something and began turning it in his paws and nibbling at it. Two wood pigeons that had been noisily courting among the thick grass started to make clumsy, fluttering love. A pair of hedge sparrows went busily on collecting bits and pieces for a nest they were tardily building in a thorn-bush. The fat thrush finally located its worm and began pulling at it, its legs braced. Bees clustered thick among the roses on the mound, and from where he was, perhaps twenty yards away from and above the mound, Bond could just hear their summery sound. It was a scene from a fairytale—the roses, the lilies of the valley, the birds and the great shafts of sunlight lancing down through the tall trees into the pool of glistening green. Bond had climbed to his hide-out at four in the morning and he had never examined so closely or for so long the transition from night to a glorious day. He suddenly felt rather foolish. Any moment now and some damned bird would come and sit on his head!

It was the pigeons that gave the first alarm. With a loud clatter they took off and dashed into the trees. All the birds followed, and the squirrel. Now the glade was quiet except for the soft hum of the bees. What had sounded the alarm? Bond's heart began to thump. His eyes hunted, quartering the glade for a clue. Something was moving among the roses. It was a tiny movement, but an extraordinary one. Slowly, inch by inch, a single thorny stem, an unnaturally straight and rather thick one, was rising through the upper branches. It went on rising until it was a clear foot above the bush. Then it stopped. There was a solitary pink rose at the tip of the stem. Separated from the bush, it looked unnatural, but only if one happened to have watched the whole process. At a casual glance it was a stray stem and nothing else. Now, silently, the petals of the rose seemed to swivel and expand, the yellow pistils drew aside and sun glinted on a glass lens the size of a shilling. The lens seemed to be looking straight at Bond but then very, very slowly, the rose-eye began to turn on its stem and continued to turn until the lens was again looking at Bond and the whole glade had been minutely surveyed. As if satisfied, the petals softly swivelled to cover the eye and very slowly the single rose descended to join the others.

Bond's breath came out with a rush. He momentarily closed his eyes to rest them. Gipsies! If that piece of machinery was any evidence, inside the mound, deep down in the earth, was certainly the most professional left-behind spy unit that had ever been devised—far more brilliant than anything England had prepared to operate in the wake of a successful German invasion, far better than what the Germans themselves had left behind in the Ardennes. A shiver of excitement and anticipation—almost of fear—ran down Bond's spine. So he had been right! But what was to be the next act?

Now, from the direction of the mound, came a thin high-pitched whine—the sound of an electric motor at very high revs. The rose bush trembled slightly. The bees took off, hovered, and settled again. Slowly, a jagged fissure formed down the centre of the big bush and smoothly widened. Now the two halves of the bush were opening like double doors. The dark aperture broadened until Bond could see the roots of the bush running into the earth on both sides of the opening doorway. The whine of machinery was louder and there was a glint of metal from the edges of the curved doors. It was like the opening of a hinged Easter egg. In a moment the two segments stood apart and the two halves of the rose bush, still alive with bees, were splayed widely open. Now the inside of the metal caisson that supported the earth and the roots of the bush were naked to the sun. There was a glint of pale electric light from the dark aperture between the curved doors. The whine of the motor had stopped. A head and shoulders appeared, and then the rest of the man. He climbed softly out and crouched, looking sharply round the glade. There was a gun—a Luger—in his hand. Satisfied, he turned and gestured into the shaft. The head and shoulders of a second man appeared. He handed up three pairs of what looked like snowshoes and ducked out of sight. The first man selected a pair and knelt and strapped them over his boots. Now he moved about more freely, leaving no footprints, for the grass flattened only momentarily under the wide mesh and then rose slowly again. Bond smiled to himself. Clever bastards!

The second man emerged. He was followed by a third. Between them they manhandled a motor-cycle out of the shaft and stood holding it slung between them by harness webbing while the first man, who was clearly the leader, knelt and strapped the snowshoes under their boots. Then, in single file, they moved off through the trees towards the road. There was something extraordinarily sinister about the way they softly high-stepped along through the shadows, lifting and carefully placing each big webbed foot in turn.

Bond let out a long sigh of released tension and laid his head softly down on the branch to relax the strain in his neck muscles. So that was the score! Even the last small detail could now be added to the file. While the two underlings were dressed in grey overalls, the leader was wearing the uniform of the Royal Corps of Signals and his motor-cycle was an olive green BSA M20 with a British Army registration number on its petrol tank. No wonder the SHAPE dispatch-rider had let him get within range. And what did the unit do with its top secret booty? Probably radioed the cream of it out at night. Instead of the periscope, a rose-stalk aerial would rise up from the bush, the pedal generator would get going deep down under the earth and off would go the high-speed cipher groups. Ciphers? There would be many good enemy secrets down that shaft if Bond could round up the unit when it was outside the hide-out. And what a chance to feed back phoney intelligence to GRU, the Soviet Military Intelligence Apparat which was presumably the control! Bond's thoughts raced.

The two underlings were coming back. They went into the shaft and the rose bush closed over it. The leader with his machine would be among the bushes on the verge of the road. Bond glanced at his watch. Six-fifty-five. Of course! He would be waiting to see if a dispatch-rider came along. Either he did not know the man he had killed was doing a weekly run, which was unlikely, or he was assuming that SHAPE would now change the routine for additional security. These were careful people. Probably their orders were to clean up as much as possible before the summer came and there were too many holidaymakers about in the forest. Then the unit might be pulled out and put back again in the winter. Who could say what the long-term plans were? Sufficient that the leader was preparing for another kill.

The minutes ticked by. At seven-ten the leader reappeared. He stood in the shadow of a big tree at the edge of the clearing and whistled once on a brief, high, birdlike note. Immediately the rose bush began to open and the two underlings came out and followed the leader back into the trees. In two minutes they were back with the motor-cycle slung between them. The leader, after a careful look round to see that they had left no traces, followed them down into the shaft and the two halves of the rose bush closed swiftly behind him.

Half an hour later life had started up in the glade again. An hour later still, when the high sun had darkened the shadows,

James Bond silently edged backwards along his branch, dropped softly on to a patch of moss behind some brambles and melted carefully back into the forest.

That evening Bond's routine call with Mary Ann Russell was a stormy one. She said: 'You're crazy. I'm not going to let you do it. I'm going to get Head of F to ring up Colonel Schreiber and tell him the whole story. This is SHAPE's job. Not yours.'

Bond said sharply: 'You'll do nothing of the sort. Colonel Schreiber says he's perfectly happy to let me make a dummy run tomorrow morning instead of the duty dispatch-rider. That's all he needs to know at this stage. Reconstruction of the crime sort of thing. He couldn't care less. He's practically closed the file on this business. Now, be a good girl and do as you're told. Just put my report on the printer to M. He'll see the point of me cleaning this thing up. He won't object.'

'Damn M! Damn you! Damn the whole silly Service!' There were angry tears in the voice. 'You're just a lot of children playing at Red Indians. Taking these people on by yourself! It's—it's showing off. That's all it is. Showing off.'

Bond was beginning to get annoyed. He said: 'That's enough, Mary Ann. Put that report on the printer. I'm sorry, but it's an order.'

There was resignation in the voice. 'Oh, all right. You don't have to pull your rank on me. But don't get hurt. At least you'll have the boys from the local Station to pick up the bits. Good luck.'

'Thanks, Mary Ann. And will you have dinner with me to-morrow night? Some place like Armenonville. Pink champagne and gipsy violins. Paris in the spring routine.'

'Yes,' she said seriously. 'I'd like that. But then take care all the more, would you? Please?'

'Of course I will. Don't worry. Goodnight.'

' 'Night.'

Bond spent the rest of the evening putting a last high polish on his plans and giving a final briefing to the four men from the Station.

It was another beautiful day. Bond, sitting comfortably astride the throbbing BSA waiting for the off, could hardly believe in the ambush that would now be waiting for him just beyond the Carrefour Royal. The corporal from the Signal Corps who had handed him his empty dispatch-case and was about to give him the signal to go said: 'You look as if you'd been in the Royal Corps all your life, sir. Time for a haircut soon, I'd say, but the uniform's bang on. How d'you like the bike, sir?'

'Goes like a dream. I'd forgotten what fun these damned things are.'

'Give me a nice little Austin A40 any day, sir.' The corporal looked at his watch. 'Seven o'clock just coming up.' He held up his thumb. 'Okay.'

Bond pulled the goggles down over his eyes, lifted a hand to the corporal, kicked the machine into gear and wheeled off across the gravel and through the main gates.

Off 184 and on to 307, through Bailly and Noisy-le-Roi and there was the straggle of St Nom. Here he would be turning sharp right on to D98—the 'route de la mort', as the handler had called it. Bond pulled into the grass verge and once more looked to the long-barrel .45 Colt. He put the warm gun back against his stomach and left the jacket button undone. On your marks! Get set . . . !

Bond took the sharp corner and accelerated up to fifty. The viaduct carrying the Paris autoroute loomed up ahead. The dark mouth of the tunnel beneath it opened and swallowed him. The noise of his exhaust was gigantic, and for an instant there was a tunnel smell of cold and damp. Then he was out in the sunshine again and immediately across the Carrefour

Royal. Ahead the oily tarmac glittered dead straight for two miles through the enchanted forest and there was a sweet smell of leaves and dew. Bond cut his speed to forty. The driving-mirror by his left hand shivered slightly with his speed. It showed nothing but an empty unfurling vista of road between lines of trees that curled away behind him like a green wake. No sign of the killer. Had he taken fright? Had there been some hitch? But then there was a tiny black speck in the centre of the convex glass—a midge that became a fly and then a bee and then a beetle. Now it was a crash helmet bent low over handlebars between two big black paws. God, he was coming fast! Bond's eyes flickered from the mirror to the road ahead and back to the mirror. When the killer's right hand went for his gun . . . !

Bond slowed—thirty-five, thirty, twenty. Ahead the tarmac was smooth as metal. A last quick look in the mirror. The right hand had left the handlebars. The sun on the man's goggles made huge fiery eyes below the rim of the crash helmet. Now! Bond braked fiercely and skidded the BSA through forty-five degrees, killing the engine. He was not quite quick enough on the draw. The killer's gun flared twice and a bullet tore into the saddle-springs beside Bond's thigh. But then the Colt spoke its single word, and the killer and his BSA, as if lassoed from within the forest, veered crazily off the road, leapt the ditch and crashed head-on into the trunk of a beech. For a moment the tangle of man and machinery clung to the broad trunk and then, with a metallic death-rattle, toppled backwards into the grass.

Bond got off his machine and walked over to the ugly twist of khaki and smoking steel. There was no need to feel for a pulse. Wherever the bullet had struck, the crash helmet had smashed like an eggshell. Bond turned away and thrust his gun back into the front of his tunic. He had been lucky. It would not do to press his luck. He got on the BSA and accelerated back down the road.

He leant the BSA up against one of the scarred trees just inside the forest and walked softly through to the edge of the clearing. He took up his stand in the shadow of the big beech. He moistened his lips and gave, as near as he could, the killer's bird-whistle. He waited. Had he got the whistle wrong? But then the bush trembled and the high thin whine began. Bond hooked his right thumb through his belt within inches of his gun-butt. He hoped he would not have to do any more killing. The two underlings had not seemed to be armed. With any luck they would come quietly.

Now the curved doors were open. From where he was, Bond could not see down the shaft, but within seconds the first man was out and putting on his snowshoes and the second followed. Snowshoes! Bond's heart missed a beat. He had forgotten them! They must be hidden back there in the bushes. Blasted fool! Would they notice?

The two men came slowly towards him, delicately placing their feet. When he was about twenty feet away, the leading man said something softly in what sounded like Russian. When Bond did not reply, the two men stopped in their tracks. They stared at him in astonishment, waiting perhaps for the answer to a password. Bond sensed trouble. He whipped out his gun and moved towards them, crouching. 'Hands up.' He gestured with the muzzle of the Colt. The leading man shouted an order and threw himself forward. At the same time the second man made a dash back towards the hideout. A rifle boomed from among the trees and the man's right leg buckled under him. The men from the Station broke cover and came running. Bond fell to one knee and clubbed upwards with his gun-barrel at the hurtling body. It made contact, but then the man was on him. Bond saw fingernails flashing towards his eyes, ducked and ran into an uppercut. Now a hand was at his right wrist and his gun was being slowly turned on him. Not wanting to kill, he had kept the safety catch up. He tried to get his thumb to it. A boot hit him in the side of the head and he let the gun go and fell back. Through a red mist he saw the muzzle of the gun pointing at his face. The thought flashed through his mind that he was going to die—die for showing mercy . . . !

Suddenly the gun muzzle had gone and the weight of the man was off him. Bond got to his knees and then to his feet. The body, spreadeagled in the grass beside him, gave a last kick. There were bloody rents in the back of the dungarees. Bond looked round. The four men from the Station were in a group. Bond undid the strap of his crash helmet and rubbed the side of his head. He said: 'Well, thanks. Who did it?'

Nobody answered. The men looked embarrassed.

Bond walked towards them, puzzled. 'What's up?'

Suddenly Bond caught a trace of movement behind the men. An extra leg showed—a woman's leg. Bond laughed out loud. The men grinned sheepishly and looked behind them. Mary Ann Russell, in a brown shirt and black jeans, came out from behind them with her hands up. One of the hands held what looked like a .22 target pistol. She brought her hands down and tucked the pistol into the top of her jeans. She came up to Bond. She said anxiously: 'You won't blame anybody, will you? I just wouldn't let them leave this morning without me.' Her eyes pleaded. 'Rather lucky I did come, really. I mean, I just happened to get to you first. No one wanted to shoot for fear of hitting you.'

Bond smiled into her eyes. He said: 'If you hadn't come, I'd have had to break that dinner date.' He turned back to the men, his voice businesslike. 'All right. One of you take the motor-bike and report the gist of this to Colonel Schreiber. Say we're waiting for his team before we take a look at the hide-out. And would he include a couple of anti-sabotage men. That shaft may be booby-trapped. All right?'

Bond took the girl by the arm. He said: 'Come over here. I want to show you a bird's nest.'

'Is that an order?'

'Yes.'

The most beautiful bird in Jamaica, and some say the most beautiful bird in the world, is the streamertail or doctor humming-bird. The cock bird is about nine inches long, but seven inches of it are tail—two long black feathers that curve and cross each other and whose inner edges are in a form of scalloped design. The head and crest are black, the wings dark green, the long bill is scarlet, and the eyes, bright and confiding, are black. The body is emerald green, so dazzling that when the sun is on the breast you see the brightest green thing in nature. In Jamaica, birds that are loved are given nicknames. *Trochilus polytmus* is called 'doctor bird' because his two black streamers remind people of the black tail-coat of the old-time physician.

Mrs Havelock was particularly devoted to two families of these birds because she had been watching them sipping honey, fighting, nesting and making love since she married and came to Content. She was now over fifty, so many generations of these two families had come and gone since the original two pairs had been nicknamed Pyramus and Thisbe and Daphnis and Chloe by her mother-in-law. But successive couples had kept the names, and Mrs Havelock now sat at her elegant tea service on the broad cool veranda and watched Pyramus, with a fierce 'tee-tee-tee' dive-bomb Daphnis who had finished up the honey on his own huge bush of Japanese

Hat and had sneaked in among the neighbouring Monkey-fiddle that was Pyramus's preserve. The two tiny black and green comets swirled away across the fine acres of lawn, dotted with brilliant clumps of hibiscus and bougainvillaea, until they were lost to sight in the citrus groves. They would soon be back. The running battle between the two families was a game. In this big finely planted garden there was enough honey for all.

Mrs Havelock put down her teacup and took a Patum Peperium sandwich. She said: 'They really are the most dreadful show-offs.'

Colonel Havelock looked over the top of his *Daily Gleaner*. 'Who?'

'Pyramus and Daphnis.'

'Oh, yes.' Colonel Havelock thought the names idiotic. He said: 'It looks to me as if Batista will be on the run soon. Castro's keeping up the pressure pretty well. Chap at Barclay's told me this morning that there's a lot of funk money coming over here already. Said that Belair's been sold to nominees. One hundred and fifty thousand pounds for a thousand acres of cattle-tick and a house the red ants'll have down by Christmas! Somebody's suddenly gone and bought that ghastly Blue Harbour hotel, and there's even talk that Jimmy Farquharson has found a buyer for his place—leaf-spot and Panama disease thrown in for good measure, I suppose.'

'That'll be nice for Ursula. The poor dear can't stand it out here. But I can't say I like the idea of the whole island being bought up by these Cubans. But Tim, where do they get all the money from, anyway?'

'Rackets, union funds, Government money—God knows. The place is riddled with crooks and gangsters. They must want to get their money out of Cuba and into something else quick. Jamaica's as good as anywhere else now we've got this convertibility with the dollar. Apparently the man who bought Belair just shovelled the money on to the floor of Aschenheim's office out of a suitcase. I suppose he'll keep the place for a year or two, and when the trouble's blown over or when Castro's got in and finished cleaning up he'll put it on the market again, take a reasonable loss and move off somewhere else. Pity, in a way. Belair used to be a fine property. It could have been brought back if anyone in the family had cared.'

'It was ten thousand acres in Bill's grandfather's day. It used to take the busher three days to ride the boundary.'

'Fat lot Bill cares. I bet he's booked his passage to London already. That's one more of the old families gone. Soon won't be anyone left of that lot but us. Thank God Judy likes the place.'

Mrs Havelock said 'Yes, dear' calmingly and pinged the bell for the tea things to be cleared away. Agatha, a huge blue-black Negress wearing the old-fashioned white headcloth that has gone out in Jamaica except in the hinterland, came out through the white and rose drawing-room followed by Fayprince, a pretty young quadroon from Port Maria whom she was training as second housemaid. Mrs Havelock said: 'It's time we started bottling, Agatha. The guavas are early this year.'

Agatha's face was impassive. She said: 'Yes'm. But we done need more bottles.'

'Why? It was only last year I got you two dozen of the best I could find at Henriques.'

'Yes'm. Someone done mash five, six of dose.'

'Oh dear. How did that happen?'

'Couldn't say'm.' Agatha picked up the big silver tray and waited, watching Mrs Havelock's face.

Mrs Havelock had not lived most of her life in Jamaica without learning that a mash is a mash and that one would not get anywhere hunting for a culprit. So she just said cheerfully:

'Oh, all right, Agatha. I'll get some more when I go into Kingston.'

'Yes'm.' Agatha, followed by the young girl, went back into the house.

Mrs Havelock picked up a piece of petit-point and began stitching, her fingers moving automatically. Her eyes went back to the big bushes of Japanese Hat and Monkeyfiddle. Yes, the two male birds were back. With gracefully cocked tails they moved among the flowers. The sun was low on the horizon and every now and then there was a flash of almost piercingly beautiful green. A mocking-bird, on the topmost branch of a frangipani, started on its evening repertoire. The tinkle of an early tree-frog announced the beginning of the short violet dusk.

Content, twenty thousand acres in the foothills of Candlefly Peak, one of the most easterly of the Blue Mountains in the county of Portland, had been given to an early Havelock by Oliver Cromwell as a reward for having been one of the signatories to King Charles's death warrant. Unlike so many other settlers of those and later times the Havelocks had maintained the plantation through three centuries, through earthquakes and hurricanes and through the boom and bust of cocoa, sugar, citrus and copra. Now it was in bananas and cattle, and it was one of the richest and best run of all the private estates in the island. The house, patched up or rebuilt after earthquake or hurricane, was a hybrid—a mahogany-pillared, two-storeyed central block on the old stone foundations flanked by two single-storeyed wings with widely overhung, flat-pitched Jamaican roofs of silver cedar shingles. The Havelocks were now sitting on the deep veranda of the central block facing the gently sloping garden beyond which a vast tumbling jungle vista stretched away twenty miles to the sea.

Colonel Havelock put down his *Gleaner.* I thought I heard a car.'

Mrs Havelock said firmly: 'If it's those ghastly Feddens from Port Antonio, you've simply got to get rid of them. I can't stand any more of their moans about England. And last time they were both quite drunk when they left and dinner was cold.' She got up quickly. 'I'm going to tell Agatha to say I've got a migraine.'

Agatha came out through the drawing-room door. She looked fussed. She was followed closely by three men. She said hurriedly: 'Gemmun from Kingston'm. To see de Colonel.'

The leading man slid past the housekeeper. He was still wearing his hat, a panama with a short very upcurled brim. He took this off with his left hand and held it against his stomach. The rays of the sun glittered on hair-grease and on a mouthful of smiling white teeth. He went up to Colonel Havelock, his outstretched hand held straight in front of him. 'Major Gonzales. From Havana. Pleased to meet you, Colonel.'

The accent was the sham American of a Jamaican taxi-driver. Colonel Havelock had got to his feet. He touched the outstretched hand briefly. He looked over the Major's shoulder at the other two men who had stationed themselves on either side of the door. They were both carrying that new holdall of the tropics—a Pan American overnight bag. The bags looked heavy. Now the two men bent down together and placed them beside their yellowish shoes. They straightened themselves. They wore flat white caps with transparent green visors that cast green shadows down to their cheekbones. Through the green shadows their intelligent animal eyes fixed themselves on the Major, reading his behaviour.

'They are my secretaries.'

Colonel Havelock took a pipe out of his pocket and began to fill it. His direct blue eyes took in the sharp clothes, the natty shoes, the glistening fingernails of the Major and the blue jeans and calypso shirts of the other two. He wondered how he could get these men into his study and near the revolver in the top drawer of his desk. He said: 'What can I do for you?' As he lit his pipe he watched the Major's eyes and mouth through the smoke.

Major Gonzales spread his hands. The width of his smile remained constant. The liquid, almost golden eyes were amused, friendly. 'It is a matter of business, Colonel. I represent a certain gentleman in Havana'—he made a throw-away gesture with his right hand. 'A powerful gentleman. A very fine guy.' Major Gonzales assumed an expression of sincerity. 'You would like him, Colonel. He asked me to present his compliments and to inquire the price of your property.'

Mrs Havelock, who had been watching the scene with a polite half-smile on her lips, moved to stand beside her husband. She said kindly, so as not to embarrass the poor man: 'What a shame, Major. All this way on these dusty roads! Your friend really should have written first, or asked anyone in Kingston or at Government House. You see, my husband's family have lived here for nearly three hundred years.' She looked at him sweetly, apologetically. 'I'm afraid there just isn't any question of selling Content. There never has been. I wonder where your important friend can possibly have got the idea from.'

Major Gonzales bowed briefly. His smiling face turned back to Colonel Havelock. He said, as if Mrs Havelock had not opened her mouth: 'My gentleman is told this is one of the finest estancias in Jamaica. He is a most generous man. You may mention any sum that is reasonable.'

Colonel Havelock said firmly: 'You heard what Mrs Havelock said. The property is not for sale.'

Major Gonzales laughed. It sounded quite genuine laughter. He shook his head as if he was explaining something to a rather dense child. 'You misunderstand me, Colonel. My gentleman desires this property and no other property in Jamaica. He has some funds, some extra funds, to invest. These funds are seeking a home in Jamaica. My gentleman wishes this to be their home.'

Colonel Havelock said patiently: 'I quite understand, Major. And I am so sorry you have wasted your time. Content will never be for sale in my lifetime. And now, if you'll forgive me. My wife and I always dine early, and you have a long way to go.' He made a gesture to the left, along the veranda. 'I think you'll find this is the quickest way to your car. Let me show you.'

Colonel Havelock moved invitingly, but when Major Gonzales stayed where he was, he stopped. The blue eyes began to freeze.

There was perhaps one less tooth in Major Gonzales's smile and his eyes had become watchful. But his manner was still jolly. He said cheerfully, 'Just one moment, Colonel.' He issued a curt order over his shoulder. Both the Havelocks noticed the jolly mask slip with the few sharp words through the teeth. For the first time Mrs Havelock looked slightly uncertain. She moved still closer to her husband. The two men picked up their blue Pan American bags and stepped forward. Major Gonzales reached for the zipper on each of them in turn and pulled. The taut mouths sprang open. The bags were full to the brim with neat solid wads of American money. Major Gonzales spread his arms. 'All hundred dollar bills. All genuine. Half a million dollars. That is, in your money, let us say, one hundred and eighty thousand pounds. A small fortune. There are many other good places to live in the world, Colonel. And perhaps my gentleman would add a further twenty thousand pounds to make the round sum. You would know in a week. All I need is half a sheet of paper with your signature. The lawyers can do the rest. Now, Colonel,' the smile was winning, 'shall we say yes and shake hands on it? Then the bags stay here and we leave you to your dinner.'

The Havelocks now looked at the Major with the same expression—a mixture of anger and disgust. One could imagine Mrs Havelock telling the story next day. 'Such a common, greasy little man. And these filthy plastic bags full of money! Timmy was wonderful. He just told him to get out and take the dirty stuff away with him.'

Colonel Havelock's mouth turned down with distaste. He said: 'I thought I had made myself clear, Major. The property is not for sale at any price. And I do not share the popular thirst for American dollars. I must now ask you to leave.' Colonel Havelock laid his cold pipe on the table as if he was preparing to roll up his sleeves.

For the first time Major Gonzales's smile lost its warmth. The mouth continued to grin but it was now shaped in an angry grimace. The liquid golden eyes were suddenly brassy and hard. He said softly: 'Colonel. It is I who have not made myself clear. Not you. My gentleman has instructed me to say that if you will not accept his most generous terms we must proceed to other measures.'

Mrs Havelock was suddenly afraid. She put her hand on Colonel Havelock's arm and pressed it hard. He put his hand over hers in reassurance. He said through tight lips: 'Please leave us alone and go, Major. Otherwise I shall communicate with the police.'

The pink tip of Major Gonzales's tongue came out and slowly licked along his lips. All the light had gone out of his face and it had become taut and hard. He said harshly. 'So the property is not for sale in your lifetime, Colonel. Is that your last word?' His right hand went behind his back and he clicked his fingers softly, once. Behind him the gun-hands of the two men slid through the opening of their gay shirts above the waistbands. The sharp animal eyes watched the Major's fingers behind his back.

Mrs Havelock's hand went up to her mouth. Colonel Havelock tried to say yes, but his mouth was dry. He swallowed noisily. He could not believe it. This mangy Cuban crook must be bluffing. He managed to say thickly: 'Yes, it is.'

Major Gonzales nodded curtly. 'In that case, Colonel, my gentleman will carry on the negotiations with the next owner—with your daughter.'

The fingers clicked. Major Gonzales stepped to one side to give a clear field of fire. The brown monkey-hands came out from under the gay shirts. The ugly sausage-shaped hunks of metal spat and thudded—again and again, even when the two bodies were on their way to the ground.

Major Gonzales bent down and verified where the bullets had hit. Then the three small men walked quickly back through the rose and white drawing-room and across the dark carved mahogany hall and out through the elegant front door. They climbed unhurriedly into a black Ford Consul Sedan with Jamaican number plates and, with Major Gonzales driving and the two gunmen sitting upright in the back seat, they drove off at an easy pace down the long avenue of Royal Palms. At the junction of the drive and the road to Port Antonio the cut telephone wires hung down through the trees like bright lianas. Major Gonzales slalomed the car carefully and expertly down the rough parochial road until he was on the metalled strip near the coast. Then he put on speed. Twenty minutes after the killing he came to the outer sprawl of the little banana port. There he ran the stolen car on to the grass verge beside the road and the three men got out and walked the quarter of a mile through the sparsely lit main street to the banana wharves. The speedboat was waiting, its exhaust bubbling. The three men got in and the boat zoomed off across the still waters of what an American poetess has called the most beautiful harbour in the world. The anchor chain was already half up on the glittering fifty-ton Chriscraft. She was flying the Stars and Stripes. The two graceful antennae of the deep-sea rods explained that these were tourists—from Kingston, perhaps, or from Montego Bay. The three men went on board and the speedboat was swung in. Two canoes were circling, begging. Major Gonzales tossed a fifty-cent piece to each of them and the stripped men dived. The twin diesels awoke to a stuttering roar and the Chriscraft settled her stern down a fraction and made for the deep channel below the Titchfield hotel. By dawn she would be back in Havana. The fishermen and wharfingers ashore watched her go, and went on with their argument as to which of the filmstars holidaying in Jamaica this could have been.

Up on the broad veranda of Content the last rays of the sun glittered on the red stains. One of the doctor birds whirred over the balustrade and hovered close above Mrs Havelock's heart, looking down. No, this was not for him. He flirted gaily off to his roosting-perch among the closing hibiscus.

There came the sound of someone in a small sports car making a racing change at the bend of the drive.

If Mrs Havelock had been alive she would have been getting ready to say: 'Judy, I'm always telling you not to do that on the corner. It scatters gravel all over the lawn and you know how it ruins Joshua's lawnmower.'

It was a month later. In London, October had begun with a week of brilliant Indian summer, and the noise of the mowers came up from Regent's Park and in through the wide open windows of M's office. They were motor-mowers and James Bond reflected that one of the most beautiful noises of summer, the drowsy iron song of the old machines, was going for ever from the world. Perhaps today children felt the same about the puff and chatter of the little two-stroke engines. At least the cut grass would smell the same.

Bond had time for these reflections because M seemed to be having difficulty in coming to the point. Bond had been asked if he had anything on at the moment, and he had replied happily that he hadn't and had waited for Pandora's box to be opened for him. He was mildly intrigued because M had addressed him as James and not by his number—007. This was unusual during duty hours. It sounded as if there might be some personal angle to this assignment—as if it might be put to him more as a request than as an order. And it seemed to Bond that there was an extra small cleft of worry between the frosty, damnably clear, grey eyes. And three minutes was certainly too long to spend getting a pipe going.

M swivelled his chair round square with the desk and flung the box of matches down so that it skidded across the red leather top towards Bond. Bond fielded it and skidded it politely back to the middle of the desk. M smiled briefly. He seemed to make up his mind. He said mildly: 'James, has it ever occurred to you that every man in the fleet knows what to do except the commanding admiral?'

Bond frowned. He said: 'It hadn't occurred to me, sir. But I see what you mean. The rest only have to carry out orders. The admiral has to decide on the orders. I suppose it's the same as saying that Supreme Command is the loneliest post there is.'

M jerked his pipe sideways. 'Same sort of idea. Someone's got to be tough. Someone's got to decide in the end. If you send a havering signal to the Admiralty you deserve to be put on the beach. Some people are religious—pass the decision on to God.' M's eyes were defensive. 'I used to try that sometimes in the Service, but He always passed the buck back again— told me to get on and make up my own mind. Good for one, I suppose, but tough. Trouble is, very few people keep tough after about forty. They've been knocked about by life—had troubles, tragedies, illnesses. These things soften you up.' M looked sharply at Bond. 'How's your coefficient of toughness, James? You haven't got to the dangerous age yet.'

Bond didn't like personal questions. He didn't know what to answer, nor what the truth was. He had not got a wife or children—had never suffered the tragedy of a personal loss. He had not had to stand up to blindness or a mortal disease. He had absolutely no idea how he would face these things that needed so much more toughness than he had ever had to show. He said hesitantly: 'I suppose I can stand most things if I have to and if I think it's right, sir. I mean'—he did not like using such words—'if the cause is—er—sort of just, sir.' He went on, feeling ashamed at himself for throwing the ball back at M: 'Of course it's not easy to know what is just and what isn't. I suppose I assume that when I'm given an unpleasant job in the Service the cause is a just one.'

'Dammit,' M's eyes glittered impatiently. 'That's just what I mean! You rely on *me*. You won't take any damned responsibility yourself.' He thrust the stem of his pipe towards his chest. 'I'm the one who has to do that. I'm the one who has to decide if a thing is right or not.' The anger died out of the eyes. The grim mouth bent sourly. He said gloomily: 'Oh well, I suppose it's what I'm paid for. Somebody's got to drive the bloody train.' M put his pipe back in his mouth and drew on it deeply to relieve his feelings.

Now Bond felt sorry for M. He had never before heard M use as strong a word as 'bloody'. Nor had M ever given a member of his staff any hint that he felt the weight of the burden he was carrying and had carried ever since he had thrown up the certain prospect of becoming Fifth Sea Lord in order to take over the Secret Service. M had got himself a problem. Bond wondered what it was. It would not be concerned with danger. If M could get the odds more or less right he would risk anything, anywhere in the world. It would not be political. M did not give a damn for the susceptibilities of any Ministry and thought nothing of going behind their backs to get a personal ruling from the Prime Minister. It might be moral. It might be personal. Bond said: 'Is there anything I can help over, sir?'

M looked briefly, thoughtfully at Bond, and then swivelled his chair so that he could look out of the window at the high summery clouds. He said abruptly: 'Do you remember the Havelock case?'

'Only what I read in the papers, sir. Elderly couple in Jamaica. The daughter came home one night and found them full of bullets. There was some talk of gangsters from Havana. The housekeeper said three men had called in a car. She thought they might have been Cubans. It turned out the car had been stolen. A yacht had sailed from the local harbour that night. But as far as I remember the police didn't get anywhere. That's all, sir. I haven't seen any signals passing on the case.'

M said gruffly: 'You wouldn't have. They've been personal to me. We weren't asked to handle the case. Just happens,' M cleared his throat: this private use of the Service was on his conscience, 'I knew the Havelocks. Matter of fact I was best man at their wedding. Malta. Nineteen-twenty-five.'

'I see, sir. That's bad.'

M said shortly: 'Nice people. Anyway, I told Station C to look into it. They didn't get anywhere with the Batista people, but we've got a good man with the other side—with this chap Castro. And Castro's Intelligence people seem to have the Government pretty well penetrated. I got the whole story a couple of weeks ago. It boils down to the fact that a man called Hammerstein, or von Hammerstein, had the couple killed. There are a lot of Germans well dug in in these banana republics. They're Nazis who got out of the net at the end of the War. This one's ex-Gestapo. He got a job as head of Batista's Counter Intelligence. Made a packet of money out of extortion and blackmail and protection. He was set up for life until Castro's lot began to make headway. He was one of the first to start easing himself out. He cut one of his officers in on his loot, a man called Gonzales, and this man travelled around the Caribbean with a couple of gunmen to protect him and began salting away Hammerstein's money outside Cuba—put it in real estate and suchlike under nominees. Only bought the best, but at top prices. Hammerstein could afford them. When money didn't work he'd use force—kidnap a child, burn down a few acres, anything to make the owner see reason. Well, this man Hammerstein heard of the Havelocks' property, one of the best in Jamaica, and he told Gonzales to go and get it. I suppose his orders were to kill the Havelocks if they wouldn't sell and then put pressure on the daughter. There's a daughter, by the way. Should be about twenty-five by now. Never seen her myself. Anyway, that's what happened. They killed the Havelocks. Then two weeks ago Batista sacked Hammerstein. May have got to hear about one of these jobs. I don't know. But, anyway, Hammerstein cleared out and took his little team of three with him. Timed things pretty well, I should say. It looks as if Castro may get in this winter if he keeps the pressure up.'

Bond said softly: 'Where have they gone to?'

'America. Right up in the North of Vermont. Up against the Canadian border. Those sort of men like being close to frontiers. Place called Echo Lake. It's some kind of a millionaire's ranch he's rented. Looks pretty from the photographs. Tucked away in the mountains with this little lake in the grounds. He's certainly chosen himself somewhere where he won't be troubled with visitors.'

'How did you get on to this, sir?'

'I sent a report of the whole case to Edgar Hoover. He knew of the man. I guessed he would. He's had a lot of trouble with this gun-running from Miami to Castro. And he's been interested in Havana ever since the big American gangster money started following the casinos there. He said that Hammerstein

and his party had come into the States on six months visitors'
visas. He was very helpful. Wanted to know if I'd got enough
to build up a case on. Did I want these men extradited for trial
in Jamaica? I talked it over here with the Attorney General and
he said there wasn't a hope unless we could get the witnesses
from Havana. There's no chance of that. It was only through
Castro's Intelligence that we even know as much as we do. Of-
ficially the Cubans won't raise a finger. Next, Hoover offered
to have their visas revoked and get them on the move again. I
thanked him and said no, and we left it at that.'

M sat for a moment in silence. His pipe had died and he
relit it. He went on: 'I decided to have a talk with our friends
the Mounties. I got on to the Commissioner on the scrambler.
He's never let me down yet. He strayed one of his frontier pa-
trol planes over the border and took a full aerial survey of this
Echo Lake place. Said that if I wanted any other cooperation
he'd provide it. And now,' M slowly swivelled his chair back
square with the desk, 'I've got to decide what to do next.'

Now Bond realized why M was troubled, why he wanted
someone else to make the decision. Because these had been
friends of M. Because a personal element was involved, M had
worked on the case by himself. And now it had come to the
point when justice ought to be done and these people brought
to book. But M was thinking: is this justice, or is it revenge?
No judge would take a murder case in which he had personally known the murdered person. M wanted someone else,
Bond, to deliver judgement. There were no doubts in Bond's
mind. He didn't know the Havelocks or care who they were.
Hammerstein had operated the law of the jungle on two de-
fenceless old people. Since no other law was available, the
law of the jungle should be visited upon Hammerstein. In no
other way could justice be done. If it was revenge, it was the
revenge of the community.

Bond said: 'I wouldn't hesitate for a minute, sir. If foreign gangsters find they can get away with this kind of thing they'll decide the English are as soft as some other people seem to think we are. This is a case for rough justice—an eye for an eye.'

M went on looking at Bond. He gave no encouragement, made no comment.

Bond said: 'These people can't be hung, sir. But they ought to be killed.'

M's eyes ceased to focus on Bond. For a moment they were blank, looking inward. Then he slowly reached for the top drawer of his desk on the left-hand side, pulled it open and extracted a thin file without the usual title across it and without the top-secret red star. He placed the file squarely in front of him and his hand rummaged again in the open drawer. The hand brought out a rubber stamp and a red-ink pad. M opened the pad, tamped the rubber stamp on it and then carefully, so that it was properly aligned with the top righthand corner of the docket, pressed it down on the grey cover.

M replaced the stamp and the ink pad in the drawer and closed the drawer. He turned the docket round and pushed it gently across the desk to Bond.

The red sanserif letters, still damp, said: FOR YOUR EYES ONLY.

Bond said nothing. He nodded and picked up the docket and walked out of the room.

Two days later, Bond took the Friday Comet to Montreal. He did not care for it. It flew too high and too fast and there were too many passengers. He regretted the days of the old Stratocruiser—that fine lumbering old plane that took ten hours to cross the Atlantic. Then one had been able to have dinner in peace, sleep for seven hours in a comfortable bunk, and get up in time to wander down to the lower deck and have that ridiculous BOAC 'country house' breakfast while the dawn came up and flooded the cabin with the first bright gold of the Western hemisphere. Now it was all too quick. The stewards had to serve everything almost at the double, and then one had a bare two hours snooze before the hundred-mile-long descent from forty thousand feet. Only eight hours after leaving London, Bond was driving a Hertz U-drive Plymouth saloon along the broad Route 17 from Montreal to Ottawa and trying to remember to keep on the right of the road.

The Headquarters of the Royal Canadian Mounted police are in the Department of Justice alongside Parliament Buildings in Ottawa. Like most Canadian public buildings, the Department of Justice is a massive block of grey masonry built to look stodgily important and to withstand the long and hard winters. Bond had been told to ask at the front desk for the Commissioner and to give his name as 'Mr James'. He did so, and a young fresh-faced RCMP corporal, who looked as if he did not like being kept indoors on a warm sunny day, took him up in the lift to the third floor and handed him over to a sergeant in a large tidy office which contained two girl secretaries and a lot of heavy furniture. The sergeant spoke on an intercom and there was a ten minutes' delay during which Bond smoked and read a recruiting pamphlet which made the Mounties sound like a mixture between a dude ranch, Dick Tracy and *Rose Marie*. When he was shown in through the connecting door a tall youngish man in a dark blue suit, white shirt and black tie turned away from the window and came towards him. 'Mr James?' the man smiled thinly. 'I'm Colonel, let's say—er—Johns.'

They shook hands. 'Come along and sit down. The Commissioner's very sorry not to be here to welcome you himself. He has a bad cold—you know, one of those diplomatic ones.' Colonel 'Johns' looked amused. 'Thought it might be best to take the day off. I'm just one of the help. I've been on one or two hunting trips myself and the Commissioner fixed on me to handle this little holiday of yours,' the Colonel paused, 'on me only. Right?'

Bond smiled. The Commissioner was glad to help but he was going to handle this with kid gloves. There would be no come-back on his office. Bond thought he must be a careful and very sensible man. He said: 'I quite understand. My friends in London didn't want the Commissioner to bother himself personally with any of this. And I haven't seen the Commissioner or been anywhere near his headquarters. That being so, can we talk English for ten minutes or so—just between the two of us?'

Colonel Johns laughed. 'Sure. I was told to make that little speech and then get down to business. You understand, Commander, that you and I are about to connive at various felonies, starting with obtaining a Canadian hunting licence under false pretences and being an accessory to a breach of the frontier laws, and going on down from there to more serious things. It wouldn't do anyone one bit of good to have any ricochets from this little lot. Get me?'

'That's how my friends feel too. When I go out of here, we'll forget each other, and if I end up in Sing-Sing that's my worry. Well, now?'

Colonel Johns opened a drawer in the desk and took out a bulging file and opened it. The top document was a list. He put his pencil on the first item and looked across at Bond. He ran his eye over Bond's old black and white hound's-tooth tweed suit and white shirt and thin black tie. He said: 'Clothes.' He unclipped a plain sheet of paper from the file and slid it across the desk. 'This is a list of what I reckon you'll need and the address of a big second-hand clothing store here in the city. Nothing fancy, nothing conspicuous— khaki shirt, dark brown jeans, good climbing boots or shoes. See they're comfortable. And there's the address of a chemist for walnut stain. Buy a gallon and give yourself a bath in the stuff. There are plenty of browns in the hills at this time and you won't want to be wearing parachute cloth or anything that smells of camouflage. Right? If you're picked up, you're an Englishman on a hunting trip in Canada who's lost his way and got across the border by mistake. Rifle. Went down myself and put it in the boot of your Plymouth while you were waiting. One of the new Savage 99Fs, Weatherby 6 x 62 'scope, five-shot repeater with twenty rounds of high-velocity .250— 3.000. Lightest big game lever action on the market. Only six and a half pounds. Belongs to a friend. Glad to have it back one day, but he won't miss it if it doesn't turn up. It's been tested and it's okay up to five hundred. Gun licence,' Colonel Johns slid it over, 'issued here in the city in your real name as that fits with your passport. Hunting licence ditto, but small game only, vermin, as it isn't quite the deer season yet, also driving licence to replace the provisional one I had waiting for you with the Hertz people. Haversack, compass—used ones, in the boot of your car. Oh, by the way,' Colonel Johns looked up from his list, 'you carrying a personal gun?'

'Yes. Walther PPK in a Burns Martin holster.'

'Right, give me the number. I've got a blank licence here. If that gets back to me it's quite okay. I've got a story for it.'

Bond took out his gun and read off the number. Colonel Johns filled in the form and pushed it over.

'Now then, maps. Here's a local Esso map that's all you need to get you to the area.' Colonel Johns got up and walked round with the map to Bond and spread it out. 'You take this route 17 back to Montreal, get on to 37 over the bridge at St Anne's and then over the river again on to 7. Follow 7 on down to Pike River. Get on 52 at Stanbridge. Turn right in Stanbridge for Frelighsburg and leave the car in a garage there. Good roads all the way. Whole trip shouldn't take you more than five hours including stops. Okay? Now this is where you've got to get things right. Make it that you get to Frelighsburg around three a.m. Garage-hand'll be half asleep and you'll be able to get the gear out of the boot and move off without him noticing even if you were a double-headed Chinaman.' Colonel Johns went back to his chair and took two more pieces of paper off the file. The first was a scrap of pencilled map, the other a section of aerial photograph. He said, looking seriously at Bond: 'Now, here are the only inflammable things you'll be carrying and I've got to rely on you getting rid of them just as soon as they've been used, or at once if there's a chance of you getting into trouble. This,' he pushed the paper over, 'is a rough sketch of an old smuggling route from Prohibition days. It's not used now or I wouldn't recommend it.' Colonel Johns smiled sourly. 'You might find some rough customers coming over in the opposite direction, and they're apt to shoot and not even ask questions afterwards—crooks, druggers, white-slavers—but nowadays they mostly travel up by Viscount. This route was used for runners between Franklin, just over the Derby Line, and Frelighsburg. You follow this path through the foothills, and you detour Franklin and get into the start of the Green Mountains. There it's all Vermont spruce and pine with a bit of maple, and you can stay inside that stuff for months and not see a soul. You get across country here, over a couple of highways, and you leave Enosburg Falls to the west. Then you're over a steep range and down into the top of the valley you want. The cross is Echo Lake and, judging from the photographs, I'd be inclined to come down on top of it from the east. Got it?'

'What's the distance? About ten miles?'

'Ten and a half. Take you about three hours from Frelighsburg if you don't lose your way, so you'll be in sight of the place around six and have about an hour's light to help you over the last stretch.' Colonel Johns pushed over the square of aerial photograph. It was a central cut from the one Bond had seen in London. It showed a long low range of well-kept buildings made of cut stone. The roofs were of slate, and there was a glimpse of graceful bow windows and a covered patio. A dust road ran past the front door and on this side were garages and what appeared to be kennels. On the garden side was a stone flagged terrace with a flowered border, and beyond this two or three acres of trim lawn stretched down to the edge of the small lake. The lake appeared to have been artificially created with a deep stone dam. There was a group of wrought-iron garden furniture where the dam wall left the bank and, halfway along the wall, a diving-board and a ladder to climb out of the lake. Beyond the lake the forest rose steeply up. It was from this side that Colonel Johns suggested an approach. There were no people in the photograph, but on the stone flags in front of the patio was a quantity of expensive-looking aluminium garden furniture and a central glass table with drinks. Bond remembered that the larger photograph had shown a tennis court in the garden and on the other side of the road the trim white fences and grazing horses of a stud farm. Echo Lake looked what it was—the luxurious retreat, in deep country, well away from atom bomb targets, of a millionaire who liked privacy and could probably offset a lot of his running expenses against the stud farm and an occasional good let. It would be an admirable refuge for a man who had had ten steamy years of Caribbean politics and who needed a rest to recharge his batteries. The lake was also convenient for washing blood off hands.

Colonel Johns closed his now empty file and tore the typewritten list into small fragments and dropped them in the wastepaper basket. The two men got to their feet. Colonel Johns took Bond to the door and held out his hand. He said: 'Well, I guess that's all. I'd give a lot to come with you. Talking about all this has reminded me of one or two sniping jobs at the end of the War. I was in the Army then. We were under

Monty in Eighth Corps. On the left of the line in the Ardennes. It was much the same sort of country as you'll be using, only different trees. But you know how it is in these police jobs. Plenty of paper work and keep your nose clean for the pension. Well, so long and the best of luck. No doubt I'll read all about it in the papers,' he smiled, 'whichever way it goes.'

Bond thanked him and shook him by the hand. A last question occurred to him. He said: 'By the way, is the Savage single pull or double? I won't have a chance of finding out and there may not be much time for experimenting when the target shows.'

'Single pull and it's a hair-trigger. Keep your finger off until you're sure you've got him. And keep outside three hundred if you can. I guess these men are pretty good themselves. Don't get too close.' He reached for the door handle. His other hand went to Bond's shoulder. 'Our Commissioner's got a motto: "Never send a man where you can send a bullet." You might remember that. So long, Commander.'

Bond spent the night and most of the next day at the KO-ZEE Motor Court outside Montreal. He paid in advance for three nights. He passed the day looking to his equipment and wearing in the soft ripple rubber climbing boots he had bought in Ottawa. He bought glucose tablets and some smoked ham and bread from which he made himself sandwiches. He also bought a large aluminium flask and filled this with three-quarters Bourbon and a quarter coffee. When darkness came he had dinner and a short sleep and then diluted the walnut stain and washed himself all over with the stuff even to the roots of his hair. He came out looking like a Red Indian with blue-grey eyes. Just before midnight he quietly opened the side door into the automobile bay, got into the Plymouth and drove off on the last lap south to Frelighsburg.

The man at the all-night garage was not as sleepy as Colonel Johns had said he would be.

'Goin' huntin', mister?'

You can get far in North America with laconic grunts. Huh, hun and hi! in their various modulations, together with sure, guess so, that so? and nuts! will meet almost any contingency.

Bond, slinging the strap of his rifle over his shoulder, said 'Hun.'

'Man got a fine beaver over by Highgate Springs Saturday.'

Bond said indifferently 'That so?', paid for two nights and walked out of the garage. He had stopped on the far side of the town, and now he only had to follow the highway for a hundred yards before he found the dirt track running off into the woods on his right. After half an hour the track petered out at a broken-down farmhouse. A chained dog set up a frenzied barking, but no light showed in the farmhouse and Bond skirted it and at once found the path by the stream. He was to follow this for three miles. He lengthened his stride to get away from the dog. When the barking stopped there was silence, the deep velvet silence of woods on a still night. It was a warm night with a full yellow moon that threw enough light down through the thick spruce for Bond to follow the path without difficulty. The springy, cushioned soles of the climbing boots were wonderful to walk on, and Bond got his second wind and knew he was making good time. At around four o'clock the trees began to thin and he was soon walking through open fields with the scattered lights of Franklin on his right. He crossed a secondary, tarred road, and now there was a wider track through the woods and on his right the pale glitter of a lake. By five o'clock he had crossed the black rivers of US highways 108 and 120. On the latter was a sign saying ENOSBURG FALLS 1 MI. Now he was on the last lap—a small hunting trail that climbed steeply. Well away from the highway, he stopped and shifted his rifle and knapsack round, had

a cigarette and burned the sketch-map. Already there was a
faint paling in the sky and small noises in the forest—the
harsh, melancholy cry of a bird he did not know and the
rustlings of small animals. Bond visualized the house deep
down in the little valley on the other side of the mountain
ahead of him. He saw the blank curtained windows, the crumpled sleeping faces of the four men, the dew on the lawn and
the widening rings of the early rise on the gunmetal surface of
the lake. And here, on the other side of the mountain, was the
executioner coming up through the trees. Bond closed his
mind to the picture, trod the remains of his cigarette into the
ground and got going.

Was this a hill or a mountain? At what height does a hill become a mountain? Why don't they manufacture something
out of the silver bark of birch trees? It looks so useful and
valuable. The best things in America are chipmunks, and oyster stew. In the evening darkness doesn't really fall, it rises.
When you sit on top of a mountain and watch the sun go
down behind the mountain opposite, the darkness rises up to
you out of the valley. Will the birds one day lose their fear of
man? It must be centuries since man has killed a small bird for
food in these woods, yet they are still afraid. Who was this
Ethan Allen who commanded the Green Mountain Boys of
Vermont? Now, in American motels, they advertise Ethan
Allen furniture as an attraction. Why? Did he make furniture?
Army boots should have rubber soles like these.

With these and other random thoughts Bond steadily
climbed upwards and obstinately pushed away from him the
thought of the four faces asleep on the white pillows.

The round peak was below the tree-line and Bond could see
nothing of the valley below. He rested and then chose an oak
tree, and climbed up and cut along a thick bough. Now he
could see everything—the endless vista of the Green Mountains stretching in every direction as far as he could see, away

to the east the golden ball of the sun just coming up in glory, and below, two thousand feet down a long easy slope of tree-tops broken once by a wide band of meadow, through a thin veil of mist, the lake, the lawns and the house.

Bond lay along the branch and watched the band of pale early morning sunshine creeping down into the valley. It took a quarter of an hour to reach the lake, and then seemed to flood at once over the glittering lawn and over the wet slate tiles of the roofs. Then the mist went quickly from the lake and the target area, washed and bright and new, lay waiting like an empty stage.

Bond slipped the telescopic sight out of his pocket and went over the scene inch by inch. Then he examined the sloping ground below him and estimated ranges. From the edge of the meadow, which would be his only open field of fire unless he went down through the last belt of trees to the edge of the lake, it would be about five hundred yards to the terrace and the patio, and about three hundred to the diving-board and the edge of the lake. What did these people do with their time? What was their routine? Did they ever bathe? It was still warm enough. Well, there was all day. If by the end of it they had not come down to the lake, he would just have to take his chance at the patio and five hundred yards. But it would not be a good chance with a strange rifle. Ought he to get on down straight away to the edge of the meadow? It was a wide meadow, perhaps five hundred yards of going without cover. It would be as well to get that behind him before the house awoke. What time did these people get up in the morning?

As if to answer him, a white blind rolled up in one of the smaller windows to the left of the main block. Bond could distinctly hear the final snap of the spring roller. Echo Lake! Of course. Did the echo work both ways? Would he have to be careful of breaking branches and twigs? Probably not. The sounds in the valley would bounce upwards off the surface of the water. But there must be no chances taken.

A thin column of smoke began to trickle up straight into the air from one of the left-hand chimneys. Bond thought of the bacon and eggs that would soon be frying. And the hot coffee. He eased himself back along the branch and down to the ground. He would have something to eat, smoke his last safe cigarette and get on down to the firing point.

The bread stuck in Bond's throat. Tension was building up in him. In his imagination he could already hear the deep bark of the Savage. He could see the black bullet lazily, like a slow flying bee, homing down into the valley towards a square of pink skin. There was a light smack as it hit. The skin dented, broke and then closed up again leaving a small hole with bruised edges. The bullet ploughed on, unhurriedly, towards the pulsing heart—the tissues, the blood-vessels, parting obediently to let it through. Who was this man he was going to do this to? What had he ever done to Bond? Bond looked thoughtfully down at his trigger finger. He crooked it slowly, feeling in his imagination the cool curve of metal. Almost automatically, his left hand reached out for the flask. He held it to his lips and tilted his head back The coffee and whisky burned a small fire down his throat. He put the top back on the flask and waited for the warmth of the whisky to reach his stomach. Then he got slowly to his feet, stretched and yawned deeply and picked up the rifle and slung it over his shoulder. He looked round carefully to mark the place when he came back up the hill and started slowly off down through the trees.

Now there was no trail and he had to pick his way slowly, watching the ground for dead branches. The trees were more mixed. Among the spruce and silver birch there was an occasional oak and beech and sycamore and, here and there, the blazing Bengal fire of a maple in autumn dress. Under the trees was a sparse undergrowth of their saplings and much dead wood from old hurricanes. Bond went carefully down, his feet making little sound among the leaves and moss-covered rocks, but soon the forest was aware of him and began to pass on the news. A large doe, with two Bambi-like young, saw him first and galloped off with an appalling clatter. A brilliant woodpecker with a scarlet head flew down ahead of him, screeching each time Bond caught up with it, and always there were the chipmunks, craning up on their hind feet, lifting their small muzzles from their teeth as they tried to catch his scent, and then scampering off to their rock holes with chatterings that seemed to fill the woods with fright. Bond willed them to have no fear, that the gun he carried was not meant for them, but with each alarm he wondered if, when he got to the edge of the meadow, he would see down on the lawn a man with glasses who had been watching the frightened birds fleeing the treetops.

But when he stopped behind a last broad oak and looked down across the long meadow to the final belt of trees and the lake and the house, nothing had changed. All the other blinds were still down and the only movement was the thin plume of smoke.

It was eight o'clock. Bond gazed down across the meadow to the trees, looking for one which would suit his purpose. He found it—a big maple, blazing with russet and crimson. This would be right for his clothes, its trunk was thick enough and it stood slightly back from the wall of spruce. From there, standing, he would be able to see all he needed of the lake and the house. Bond stood for a while, plotting his route down through the thick grass and golden-rod of the meadow. He would have to do it on his stomach, and slowly. A small breeze got up and combed the meadow. If only it would keep blowing and cover his passage!

Somewhere not far off, up to the left on the edge of the trees, a branch snapped. It snapped once decisively and there was no further noise. Bond dropped to one knee, his ears pricked and his senses questing. He stayed like that for a full ten minutes, a motionless brown shadow against the wide trunk of the oak.

Animals and birds do not break twigs. Dead wood must carry a special danger signal for them. Birds never alight on twigs that will break under them, and even a large animal like a deer with antlers and four hooves to manipulate moves quite silently in a forest unless he is in flight. Had these people after all got guards out? Gently Bond eased the rifle off his shoulder and put his thumb on the safe. Perhaps, if the people were still sleeping, a single shot, from high up in the woods, would pass for a hunter or a poacher. But then, between him and approximately where the twig had snapped, two deer broke cover and cantered unhurriedly across the meadow to the left. It was true that they stopped twice to look back, but each time they cropped a few mouthfuls of grass before moving on and into the distant fringe of the lower woods. They showed no fright and no haste. It was certainly they who had been the cause of the snapped branch. Bond breathed a sigh. So much for that. And now to get on across the meadow.

A five-hundred-yard crawl through tall concealing grass is a long and wearisome business. It is hard on knees and hands and elbows, there is a vista of nothing but grass and flower stalks, and the dust and small insects get into your eyes and nose and down your neck. Bond focused on placing his hands right and maintaining a slow, even speed. The breeze had kept up and his wake through the grass would certainly not be noticeable from the house.

From above, it looked as if a big ground animal—a beaver perhaps, or a woodchuck—was on its way down the meadow. No, it would not be a beaver. They always move in pairs. And yet perhaps it might be a beaver—for now, from higher up on the meadow, something, somebody else had entered the tall grass, and behind and above Bond a second wake was being cut in the deep sea of grass. It looked as if whatever it was would slowly catch up on Bond and that the two wakes would converge just at the next tree-line.

Bond crawled and slithered steadily on, stopping only to wipe the sweat and dust off his face and, from time to time, to make sure that he was on course for the maple. But when he was close enough for the treeline to hide him from the house, perhaps twenty feet from the maple, he stopped and lay for a while, massaging his knees and loosening his wrists for the last lap.

He had heard nothing to warn him, and when the soft threatening whisper came from only feet away in the thick grass on his left, his head swivelled so sharply that the vertebrae of his neck made a cracking sound.

'Move an inch and I'll kill you.' It had been a girl's voice, but a voice that fiercely meant what it said.

Bond, his heart thumping, stared up the shaft of the steel arrow whose blue-tempered triangular tip parted the grass stalks perhaps eighteen inches from his head.

The bow was held sideways, flat in the grass. The knuckles of the brown fingers that held the binding of the bow below the arrow-tip were white. Then there was the length of glinting steel and, behind the metal feathers, partly obscured by waving strands of grass, were grimly clamped lips below two fierce grey eyes against a background of sunburned skin damp with sweat. That was all Bond could make out through the grass. Who the hell was this? One of the guards? Bond gathered saliva back into his dry mouth and began slowly to edge his right hand, his out-of-sight hand, round and up towards his waistband and his gun. He said softly: 'Who the hell are you?'

The arrow-tip gestured threateningly. 'Stop that right hand

or I'll put this through your shoulder. Are you one of the guards?'

'No. Are you?'

'Don't be a fool. What are you doing here?' The tension in the voice had slackened, but it was still hard, suspicious. There was a trace of accent—what was it, Scots? Welsh?

It was time to get to level terms. There was something particularly deadly about the blue arrow-tip. Bond said easily: 'Put away your bow and arrow, Robina. Then I'll tell you.'

'You swear not to go for your gun?'

'All right. But for God's sake let's get out of the middle of this field.' Without waiting, Bond rose on hands and knees and started to crawl again. Now he must get the initiative and hold it. Whoever this damned girl was, she would have to be disposed of quickly and discreetly before the shooting match began. God, as if there wasn't enough to think of already!

Bond reached the trunk of the tree. He got carefully to his feet and took a quick look through the blazing leaves. Most of the blinds had gone up. Two slow-moving coloured maids were laying a large breakfast table on the patio. He had been right. The field of vision over the tops of the trees that now fell sharply to the lake was perfect. Bond unslung his rifle and knapsack and sat down with his back against the trunk of the tree. The girl came out of the edge of the grass and stood up under the maple. She kept her distance. The arrow was still held in the bow but the bow was unpulled. They looked warily at each other.

The girl looked like a beautiful unkempt dryad in ragged shirt and trousers. The shirt and trousers were olive green, crumpled and splashed with mud and stains and torn in places, and she had bound her pale blonde hair with goldenrod to conceal its brightness for her crawl through the meadow. The beauty of her face was wild and rather animal, with a wide sensuous mouth, high cheekbones and silvery grey, disdainful eyes. There was the blood of scratches on her forearms and down one cheek, and a bruise had puffed and slightly blackened the same cheekbone. The metal feathers of a quiver full of arrows showed above her left shoulder. Apart from the bow, she carried nothing but a hunting knife at her belt and, at her other hip, a small brown canvas bag that presumably carried her food. She looked like a beautiful, dangerous customer who knew wild country and forests and was not afraid of them. She would walk alone through life and have little use for civilization.

Bond thought she was wonderful. He smiled at her. He said softly, reassuringly: 'I suppose you're Robina Hood. My name's James Bond.' He reached for his flask and unscrewed the top and held it out. 'Sit down and have a drink of this— firewater and coffee. And I've got some biltong. Or do you live on dew and berries?'

She came a little closer and sat down a yard from him. She sat like a Red Indian, her knees splayed wide and her ankles tucked up high under her thighs. She reached for the flask and drank deeply with her head thrown back. She handed it back without comment. She did not smile. She said 'Thanks' grudgingly, and took her arrow and thrust it over her back to join the others in the quiver. She said, watching him closely: 'I suppose you're a poacher. The deer-hunting season doesn't open for another three weeks. But you won't find any deer down here. They only come so low at night. You ought to be higher up during the day, much higher. If you like, I'll tell you where there are some. Quite a big herd. It's a bit late in the day, but you could still get to them. They're up-wind from here and you seem to know about stalking. You don't make much noise.'

'Is that what you're doing here—hunting? Let's see your licence.'

Her shirt had buttoned-down breast pockets. Without protest she took out from one of them the white paper and handed it over.

The licence had been issued in Bennington, Vermont. It had been issued in the name of Judy Havelock. There was a list of types of permit. 'Non-resident hunting' and 'Non-resident bow and arrow' had been ticked. The cost had been $18.50, payable to the Fish and Game Service, Montpelier, Vermont. Judy Havelock had given her age as twenty-five and her place of birth as Jamaica.

Bond thought: 'God Almighty!' He handed the paper back. So that was the score! He said with sympathy and respect: 'You're quite a girl, Judy. It's a long walk from Jamaica. And you were going to take him on with your bow and arrow. You know what they say in China: "Before you set out on revenge, dig two graves." Have you done that, or did you expect to get away with it?'

The girl was staring at him. 'Who are you? What are you doing here? What do you know about it?'

Bond reflected. There was only one way out of this mess and that was to join forces with the girl. What a hell of a business! He said resignedly: 'I've told you my name. I've been sent out from London by, er, Scotland Yard. I know all about your troubles and I've come out here to pay off some of the score and see you're not bothered by these people. In London we think that the man in that house might start putting pressure on you, about your property, and there's no other way of stopping him.'

The girl said bitterly: 'I had a favourite pony, a Palomino. Three weeks ago they poisoned it. Then they shot my Alsatian. I'd raised it from a puppy. Then came a letter. It said, "Death has many hands. One of these hands is now raised over you." I was to put a notice in the paper, in the personal column, on a particular day. I was just to say, "I will obey.

Judy." I went to the police. All they did was to offer me protection. It was people in Cuba, they thought. There was nothing else they could do about it. So I went to Cuba and stayed
in the best hotel and gambled big in the casinos.' She gave a
little smile. 'I wasn't dressed like this. I wore my best dresses
and the family jewels. And people made up to me. I was nice
to them. I had to be. And all the while I asked questions. I pre-
tended I was out for thrills—that I wanted to see the under-
world and some real gangsters, and so on. And in the end I
found out about this man.' She gestured down towards the
house. 'He had left Cuba. Batista had found out about him or
something. And he had a lot of enemies. I was told plenty
about him and in the end I met a man, a sort of high-up policeman, who told me the rest after I had,' she hesitated and
avoided Bond's eyes, 'after I had made up to him.' She
paused. She went on: 'I left and went to America. I had read
somewhere about Pinkerton's, the detective people. I went to
them and paid to have them find this man's address.' She
turned her hands palm upwards on her lap. Now her eyes
were defiant. 'That's all.'

'How did you get here?'

'I flew up to Bennington. Then I walked. Four days. Up
through the Green Mountains. I kept out of the way of people.
I'm used to this sort of thing. Our house is in the mountains
in Jamaica. They're much more difficult than these. And there
are more people, peasants, about in them. Here no one ever
seems to walk. They go by car.'

'And what were you going to do then?'

'I'm going to shoot von Hammerstein and walk back to Bennington.' The voice was as casual as if she had said she was
going to pick a wild flower.

From down in the valley came the sound of voices. Bond
got to his feet and took a quick look through the branches.
Three men and two girls had come on to the patio. There was

talk and laughter as they pulled out chairs and sat down at the
table. One place was left empty at the head of the table between the two girls. Bond took out his telescopic sight and
looked through it. The three men were very small and dark.
One of them, who smiled all the time and whose clothes
looked the cleanest and smartest, would be Gonzales. The
other two were low peasant types. They sat together at the foot
of the oblong table and took no part in the talk. The girls were
swarthy brunettes. They looked like cheap Cuban whores.
They wore bright bathing dresses and a lot of gold jewellery,
and laughed and chattered like pretty monkeys. The voices
were almost clear enough to understand, but they were talking Spanish.

Bond felt the girl near him. She stood a yard behind him.
Bond handed her the glass. He said: 'The neat little man is
called Major Gonzales. The two at the bottom of the table are
gunmen. I don't know who the girls are. Von Hammerstein
isn't there yet.' She took a quick look through the glass and
handed it back without comment. Bond wondered if she realized that she had been looking at the murderers of her father
and mother.

The two girls had turned and were looking towards the door
into the house. One of them called out something that might
have been a greeting. A short, square, almost naked man came
out into the sunshine. He walked silently past the table to the
edge of the flagged terrace facing the lawn and proceeded to
go through a five-minute programme of physical drill.

Bond examined the man minutely. He was about five feet
four with a boxer's shoulders and hips, but a stomach that was
going to fat. A mat of black hair covered his breasts and shoulder blades, and his arms and legs were thick with it. By contrast, there was not a hair on his face or head and his skull was
a glittering whitish yellow with a deep dent at the back that
might have been a wound or the scar of a trepanning. The

bone structure of the face was that of the conventional Prussian officer—square, hard and thrusting—but the eyes under the naked brows were close-set and piggish, and the large mouth had hideous lips—thick and wet and crimson. He wore nothing but a strip of black material, hardly larger than an athletic support-belt, round his stomach, and a large gold wristwatch on a gold bracelet. Bond handed the glass to the girl. He was relieved. Von Hammerstein looked just about as unpleasant as M's dossier said he was.

Bond watched the girl's face. The mouth looked grim, almost cruel, as she looked down on the man she had come to kill. What was he to do about her? He could see nothing but a vista of troubles from her presence. She might even interfere with his own plans and insist on playing some silly rôle with her bow and arrow. Bond made up his mind. He just could not afford to take chances. One short tap at the base of the skull and he would gag her and tie her up until it was all over. Bond reached softly for the butt of his automatic.

Nonchalantly the girl moved a few steps back. Just as nonchalantly she bent down, put the glass on the ground and picked up her bow. She reached behind her for an arrow, and fitted it casually into the bow. Then she looked up at Bond and said quietly: 'Don't get any silly ideas. And keep your distance. I've got what's called wide-angled vision. I haven't come all the way here to be knocked on the head by a flat-footed London bobby. I can't miss with this at fifty yards, and I've killed birds on the wing at a hundred. I don't want to put an arrow through your leg, but I shall if you interfere.'

Bond cursed his previous indecision. He said fiercely: 'Don't be a silly bitch. Put that damned thing down. This is man's work. How in hell do you think you can take on four men with a bow and arrow?'

The girl's eyes blazed obstinately. She moved her right foot back into the shooting stance. She said through compressed, angry lips: 'You go to hell. And keep out of this. It was my mother and father they killed. Not yours. I've already been here a day and a night. I know what they do and I know how to get Hammerstein. I don't care about the others. They're nothing without him. Now then.' She pulled the bow half taut. The arrow pointed at Bond's feet. 'Either you do what I say or you're going to be sorry. And don't think I don't mean it. This is a private thing I've sworn to do and nobody's going to stop me.' She tossed her head imperiously. 'Well?'

Bond gloomily measured the situation. He looked the ridiculously beautiful wild girl up and down. This was good hard English stock spiced with the hot peppers of a tropical childhood. Dangerous mixture. She had keyed herself up to a state of controlled hysteria. He was quite certain that she would think nothing of putting him out of action. And he had absolutely no defence. Her weapon was silent, his would alert the whole neighbourhood. Now the only hope would be to work with her. Give her part of the job and he would do the rest. He said quietly: 'Now listen, Judy. If you insist on coming in on this thing we'd better do it together. Then perhaps we can bring it off and stay alive. This sort of thing is my profession. I was ordered to do it—by a close friend of your family, if you want to know. And I've got the right weapon. It's got at least five times the range of yours. I could take a good chance of killing him now, on the patio. But the odds aren't quite good enough. Some of them have got bathing things on. They'll be coming down to the lake. Then I'm going to do it. You can give supporting fire.' He ended lamely: 'It'll be a great help.'

'No.' She shook her head decisively. 'I'm sorry. You can give what you call supporting fire if you like. I don't care one way or the other. You're right about the swimming. Yesterday they were all down at the lake around eleven. It's just as warm today and they'll be there again. I shall get him from the edge of the trees by the lake. I found a perfect place last night. The bodyguard men bring their guns with them—sort of tommy-gun things. They don't bathe. They sit around and keep guard. I know the moment to get von Hammerstein and I'll be well away from the lake before they take in what's happened. I tell you I've got it all planned. Now then. I can't hang around any more. I ought to have been in my place already. I'm sorry, but unless you say yes straight away there's no alternative.' She raised the bow a few inches.

Bond thought: 'Damn this girl to hell.' He said angrily: 'All right then. But I can tell you that if we get out of this you're going to get such a spanking you won't be able to sit down for a week.' He shrugged. He said with resignation: 'Go ahead. I'll look after the others. If you get away all right, meet me here. If you don't, I'll come down and pick up the pieces.'

The girl unstrung her bow. She said indifferently: 'I'm glad you're seeing sense. These arrows are difficult to pull out. Don't worry about me. But keep out of sight and mind the sun doesn't catch that glass of yours.' She gave Bond the brief, pitying, self-congratulatory smile of the woman who has had the last word, and turned and made off down through the trees.

Bond watched the lithe dark green figure until it had vanished among the tree-trunks, then he impatiently picked up the glass and went back to his vantage-point. To hell with her! It was time to clear the silly bitch out of his mind and concentrate on the job. Was there anything else he could have done—any other way of handling it? Now he was committed to wait for her to fire the first shot. That was bad. But if he fired first there was no way of knowing what the hot-headed bitch would do. Bond's mind luxuriated briefly in the thought of what he would do to the girl once all this was over. Then there was movement in front of the house, and he put the exciting thoughts aside and lifted his glass.

The breakfast things were being cleared away by the two maids. There was no sign of the girls or the gunmen. Von Hammerstein was lying back among the cushions of an outdoor couch reading a newspaper and occasionally commenting to Major Gonzales, who sat astride an iron garden chair near his feet. Gonzales was smoking a cigar and from time to time he delicately raised a hand in front of his mouth, leant sideways and spat a bit of leaf out on the ground. Bond could not hear what von Hammerstein was saying, but his comments were in English and Gonzales answered in English. Bond glanced at his watch. It was ten-thirty. Since the scene seemed to be static, Bond sat down with his back to the tree and went over the Savage with minute care. At the same time he thought of what would shortly have to be done with it.

Bond did not like what he was going to do, and all the way from England he had had to keep on reminding himself what sort of men these were. The killing of the Havelocks had been a particularly dreadful killing. Von Hammerstein and his gunmen were particularly dreadful men whom many people around the world would probably be very glad to destroy, as this girl proposed to do, out of private revenge. But for Bond it was different. He had no personal motives against them. This was merely his job—as it was the job of a pest control officer to kill rats. He was the public executioner appointed by M to represent the community. In a way, Bond argued to himself, these men were as much enemies of his country as were the agents of SMERSH or of other enemy Secret Services. They had declared and waged war against British people on British soil and they were currently planning another attack. Bond's mind hunted round for more arguments to bolster his resolve. They had killed the girl's pony and her dog with two casual sideswipes of the hand as if they had been flies. They . . .

A burst of automatic fire from the valley brought Bond to

his feet. His rifle was up and taking aim as the second burst
came. The harsh racket of noise was followed by laughter and
hand-clapping. The kingfisher, a handful of tattered blue and
grey feathers, thudded to the lawn and lay fluttering. Von
Hammerstein, smoke still dribbling from the snout of his
tommy-gun, walked a few steps and put the heel of his naked
foot down and pivoted sharply. He took his heel away and
wiped it on the grass beside the heap of feathers. The others
stood round, laughing and applauding obsequiously. Von
Hammerstein's red lips grinned with pleasure. He said something which included the word 'crackshot'. He handed the
gun to one of the gunmen and wiped his hands down his fat
backsides. He gave a sharp order to the two girls, who ran off
into the house, then, with the others following, he turned and
ambled down the sloping lawn towards the lake. Now the
girls came running back out of the house. Each one carried an
empty champagne bottle. Chattering and laughing they
skipped down after the men.

Bond got himself ready. He clipped the telescopic sight on
to the barrel of the Savage and took his stance against the
trunk of the tree. He found a bump in the wood as a rest for
his left hand, put his sights at 300, and took broad aim at the
group of people by the lake. Then, holding the rifle loosely, he
leaned against the trunk and watched the scene.

It was going to be some kind of a shooting contest between
the two gunmen. They snapped fresh magazines on to their
guns and at Gonzales's orders stationed themselves on the flat
stone wall of the dam some twenty feet apart on either side of
the diving-board. They stood with their backs to the lake and
their guns at the ready.

Von Hammerstein took up his place on the grass verge, a
champagne bottle swinging in each hand. The girls stood behind him, their hands over their ears. There was excited jab-
bering in Spanish, and laughter in which the two gunmen did

not join. Through the telescopic sight their faces looked sharp with concentration.

Von Hammerstein barked an order and there was silence. He swung both arms back and counted 'Un . . . Dos . . . Tres.' With the 'tres' he hurled the champagne bottles high into the air over the lake.

The two men turned like marionettes, the guns clamped to their hips. As they completed the turn they fired. The thunder of the guns split the peaceful scene and racketed up from the water. Birds fled away from the trees screeching and some small branches cut by the bullets pattered down into the lake. The left-hand bottle disintegrated into dust, the right-hand one, hit by only a single bullet, split in two a fraction of a second later. The fragments of glass made small splashes over the middle of the lake. The gunman on the left had won. The smoke-clouds over the two of them joined and drifted away over the lawn. The echoes boomed softly into silence. The two gunmen walked along the wall to the grass the rear one looking sullen, the leading one with a sly grin on his face. Von Hammerstein beckoned the two girls forward. They came reluctantly, dragging their feet and pouting. Von Hammerstein said something, asked a question of the winner. The man nodded at the girl on the left. She looked sullenly back at him. Gonzales and Hammerstein laughed. Hammerstein reached out and patted the girl on the rump as if she had been a cow. He said something in which Bond caught the words 'una noche'. The girl looked up at him and nodded obediently. The group broke up. The prize girl took a quick run and dived into the lake, perhaps to get away from the man who had won her favours, and the other girl followed her. They swam away across the lake calling angrily to each other. Major Gonzales took off his coat and laid it on the grass and sat down on it. He was wearing a shoulder holster which showed the butt of a medium-calibre automatic. He watched von Hammerstein take off his watch and walk along the dam wall to the diving-board. The gunmen stood back from the lake and also watched von Hammerstein and the two girls, who were now out in the middle of the little lake and were making for the far shore. The gunmen stood with their guns cradled in their arms and occasionally one of them would glance round the garden or towards the house. Bond thought there was every reason why von Hammerstein had managed to stay alive so long. He was a man who took trouble to do so.

Von Hammerstein had reached the diving-board. He walked along to the end and stood looking down at the water. Bond tensed himself and put up the safe. His eyes were fierce slits. It would be any minute now. His finger itched on the trigger-guard. What in hell was the girl waiting for?

Von Hammerstein had made up his mind. He flexed his knees slightly. The arms came back. Through the telescopic sight Bond could see the thick hair over his shoulder blades tremble in a breeze that came to give a quick shiver to the surface of the lake. Now his arms were coming forward and there was a fraction of a second when his feet had left the board and he was still almost upright. In that fraction of a second there was a flash of silver against his back and then von Hammerstein's body hit the water in a neat dive.

Gonzales was on his feet, looking uncertainly at the turbulence caused by the dive. His mouth was open, waiting. He did not know if he had seen something or not. The two gunmen were more certain. They had their guns at the ready. They crouched, looking from Gonzales to the trees behind the dam, waiting for an order.

Slowly the turbulence subsided and the ripples spread across the lake. The dive had gone deep.

Bond's mouth was dry. He licked his lips, searching the lake with his glass. There was a pink shimmer deep down. It wobbled slowly up. Von Hammerstein's body broke the surface. It

lay head down, wallowing softly. A foot or so of steel shaft
stuck up from below the left shoulder blade and the sun
winked on the aluminium feathers.

Major Gonzales yelled an order and the two tommy-guns
roared and flamed. Bond could hear the crash of the bullets
among the trees below him. The Savage shuddered against
his shoulder and the right-hand man fell slowly forward on
his face. Now the other man was running for the lake, his gun
still firing from the hip in short bursts. Bond fired and missed
and fired again. The man's legs buckled, but his momentum
still carried him forward. He crashed into the water. The
clenched finger went on firing the gun aimlessly up towards
the blue sky until the water throttled the mechanism.

The seconds wasted on the extra shot had given Major Gonzales a chance. He had got behind the body of the first gunman and now he opened up on Bond with the tommy-gun.
Whether he had seen Bond or was only firing at the flashes
from the Savage he was doing well. Bullets zipped into the
maple and slivers of wood spattered into Bond's face. Bond
fired twice. The dead body of the gunman jerked. Too low!
Bond reloaded and took fresh aim. A snapped branch fell
across his rifle. He shook it free, but now Gonzales was up and
running forward to the group of garden furniture. He hurled
the iron table on its side and got behind it as two snap shots
from Bond kicked chunks out of the lawn at his heels. With
this solid cover his shooting became more accurate, and burst
after burst, now from the right of the table and now from the
left, crashed into the maple tree while Bond's single shots
clanged against the white iron or whined off across the lawn.
It was not easy to traverse the telescopic sight quickly from
one side of the table to the other and Gonzales was cunning
with his changes. Again and again his bullets thudded into
the trunk beside and above Bond. Bond ducked and ran
swiftly to the right. He would fire, standing, from the open

meadow and catch Gonzales off guard. But even as he ran, he saw Gonzales dart from behind the iron table. He also had decided to end the stalemate. He was running for the dam to get across and into the woods and come up after Bond. Bond stood and threw up his rifle. As he did so, Gonzales also saw him. He went down on one knee on the dam wall and sprayed a burst at Bond. Bond stood icily, hearing the bullets.

The crossed hairs centred on Gonzales's chest. Bond squeezed the trigger. Gonzales rocked. He half got to his feet. He raised his arms and, with his gun still pumping bullets into the sky, dived clumsily face forward into the water.

Bond watched to see if the face would rise. It did not. Slowly he lowered his rifle and wiped the back of his arm across his face.

The echoes, the echoes of much death, rolled to and fro across the valley. Away to the right, in the trees beyond the lake, he caught a glimpse of the two girls running up towards the house. Soon they, if the maids had not already done so, would be on to the state troopers. It was time to get moving.

Bond walked back through the meadow to the lone maple. The girl was there. She stood up against the trunk of the tree with her back to him. Her head was cradled in her arms against the tree. Blood was running down the right arm and dripping to the ground, and there was a black stain high up on the sleeve of the dark green shirt. The bow and quiver of arrows lay at her feet. Her shoulders were shaking.

Bond came up behind her and put a protective arm across her shoulders. He said softly: 'Take it easy, Judy. It's all over now. How bad's the arm?'

She said in a muffled voice: 'It's nothing. Something hit me. But that was awful. I didn't—I didn't know it would be like that.'

Bond pressed her arm reassuringly. 'It had to be done. They'd have got you otherwise. Those were pro killers—the worst. But I told you this sort of thing was man's work. Now then, let's have a look at your arm. We've got to get going—over the border. The troopers'll be here before long.'

She turned. The beautiful wild face was streaked with sweat and tears. Now the grey eyes were soft and obedient. She said: 'It's nice of you to be like that. After the way I was. I was sort of—sort of wound up.'

She held out her arm. Bond reached for the hunting-knife at her belt and cut off her shirtsleeve at the shoulder. There was the bruised, bleeding gash of a bullet wound across the muscle. Bond took out his own khaki handkerchief, cut it into three lengths and joined them together. He washed the wound clean with the coffee and whisky, and then took a thick slice of bread from his haversack and bound it over the wound. He cut her shirtsleeve into a sling and reached behind her neck to tie the knot. Her mouth was inches from his. The scent of her body had a warm animal tang. Bond kissed her once softly on the lips and once again, hard. He tied the knot. He looked into the grey eyes close to his. They looked surprised and happy. He kissed her again at each corner of the mouth and the mouth slowly smiled. Bond stood away from her and smiled back. He softly picked up her right hand and slipped the wrist into the sling. She said docilely: 'Where are you taking me?'

Bond said: 'I'm taking you to London. There's this old man who will want to see you. But first we've got to get over into Canada, and I'll talk to a friend in Ottawa and get your passport straightened out. You'll have to get some clothes and things. It'll take a few days. We'll be staying in a place called the KO-ZEE Motel.'

She looked at him. She was a different girl. She said softly: 'That'll be nice. I've never stayed in a motel.'

Bond bent down and picked up his rifle and knapsack and slung them over one shoulder. Then he hung her bow and quiver over the other, and turned and started up through the meadow.

She fell in behind and followed him, and as she walked she pulled the tired bits of golden-rod out of her hair and undid a ribbon and let the pale gold hair fall down to her shoulders.

James Bond said: 'I've always thought that if I ever married I would marry an air hostess.'

The dinner party had been rather sticky and now that the other two guests had left accompanied by the ADC to catch their plane, the Governor and Bond were sitting together on a chintzy sofa in the large Office of Works furnished drawing-room, trying to make conversation. Bond had a sharp sense of the ridiculous. He was never comfortable sitting deep in soft cushions. He preferred to sit up in a solidly upholstered armed chair with his feet firmly on the ground. And he felt foolish sitting with an elderly bachelor on his bed of rose chintz gazing at the coffee and liqueurs on the low table between their outstretched feet. There was something clubable, intimate, even rather feminine, about the scene and none of these atmospheres was appropriate.

Bond didn't like Nassau. Everyone was too rich. The winter visitors and the residents who had houses on the island talked of nothing but their money, their diseases and their servant problems. They didn't even gossip well. There was nothing to gossip about. The winter crowd were all too old to have love affairs and, like most rich people, too cautious to say anything malicious about their neighbours. The Harvey Millers, the couple that had just left, were typical—a pleasant rather dull Canadian millionaire who had got into Natural Gas early on and stayed with it, and his pretty chatterbox of a wife. It seemed that she was English. She had sat next to Bond and chattered vivaciously about 'what shows he had recently seen in town' and 'didn't he think the Savoy Grill was the nicest place for supper. One saw so many interesting people— actresses and people like that'. Bond had done his best, but since he had not seen a play for two years, and then only because the man he was following in Vienna had gone to it, he had had to rely on rather dusty memories of London night life which somehow failed to marry up with the experiences of Mrs Harvey Miller.

Bond knew that the Governor had asked him to dinner only as a duty, and perhaps to help out with the Harvey Millers. Bond had been in the Colony for a week and was leaving for Miami the next day. It had been a routine investigation job. Arms were getting to the Castro rebels in Cuba from all the neighbouring territories. They had been coming principally from Miami and the Gulf of Mexico, but when the US Coast Guard had seized two big shipments, the Castro supporters had turned to Jamaica and the Bahamas as possible bases, and Bond had been sent out from London to put a stop to it. He hadn't wanted to do the job. If anything, his sympathies were with the rebels, but the Government had a big export programme with Cuba in exchange for taking more Cuban sugar than they wanted, and a minor condition of the deal was that Britain should not give aid or comfort to the Cuban rebels. Bond had found out about the two big cabin cruisers that were being fitted out for the job, and rather than make arrests when they were about to sail, thus causing an incident, he had chosen a very dark night and crept up on the boats in a police launch. From the deck of the unlighted launch he had tossed a thermite bomb through an open port of each of them. He had then made off at high speed and watched the bonfire from a distance. Bad luck on the insurance companies, of course, but there were no casualties and he had achieved quickly and neatly what M had told him to do.

So far as Bond was aware, no one in the Colony, except the Chief of Police and two of his officers, knew who had caused the two spectacular, and—to those in the know— timely fires in the roadstead. Bond had reported only to M in London. He had not wished to embarrass the Governor, who seemed to him an easily embarrassable man, and it could in fact have been unwise to give him knowledge of a felony which might easily be the subject of a question in the Legislative Council. But the Governor was no fool. He had known the purpose of Bond's visit to the Colony, and that evening, when Bond had shaken him by the hand, the dis- like of a peaceable man for violent action had been commu- nicated to Bond by something constrained and defensive in the Governor's manner.

This had been no help to the dinner party, and it had needed all the chatter and gush of a hard-working ADC to give the evening the small semblance of life it had achieved.

And now it was only nine-thirty, and the Governor and Bond were faced with one more polite hour before they could go gratefully to their beds, each relieved that he would never have to see the other again. Not that Bond had anything against the Governor. He belonged to a routine type that Bond had often encountered round the world—solid, loyal, compe- tent, sober and just: the best type of Colonial Civil Servant. Solidly, competently, loyally he would have filled the minor posts for thirty years while the Empire crumbled around him; and now, just in time, by sticking to the ladders and avoiding the snakes, he had got to the top. In a year or two it would be the GCB and out—out to Godalming or Cheltenham or Tun- bridge Wells with a pension and a small packet of memories of places like the Trucial Oman, the Leeward Islands, British Guiana, that no one at the local golf club would have heard of or would care about. And yet, Bond had reflected that evening, how many small dramas such as the affair of the Castro rebels must the Governor have witnessed or been privy to! How much he would know about the chequerboard of the small-power politics, the scandalous side of life in small communities abroad, the secrets of people that lie in the files of Government Houses round the world. But how could one strike a spark off this rigid, discreet mind? How could he, James Bond, whom the Governor obviously regarded as a dangerous man and as a possible source of danger to his own career, extract one ounce of interesting fact or comment to save the evening from being a futile waste of time?

Bond's careless and slightly mendacious remark about marrying an air hostess had come at the end of some desultory conversation about air travel that had followed dully, inevitably, on the departure of the Harvey Millers to catch their plane for Montreal. The Governor had said that BOAC were getting the lion's share of the American traffic to Nassau because, though their planes might be half an hour slower from Idlewild, the service was superb. Bond had said, boring himself with his own banality, that he would rather fly slowly and comfortably than fast and uncosseted. It was then that he had made the remark about air hostesses.

'Indeed,' said the Governor in the polite, controlled voice that Bond prayed might relax and become human. 'Why?'

'Oh, I don't know. It would be fine to have a pretty girl always tucking you up and bringing you drinks and hot meals and asking if you had everything you wanted. And they're always smiling and wanting to please. If I don't marry an air hostess, there'll be nothing for it but marry a Japanese. They seem to have the right ideas too.' Bond had no intention of marrying anyone. If he did, it would certainly not be an insipid slave. He only hoped to amuse or outrage the Governor into a discussion of some human topic.

'I don't know about the Japanese, but I suppose it has occurred to you that these air hostesses are only *trained* to please, that they might be quite different when they're not on the job, so to speak.' The Governor's voice was reasonable, judicious.

'Since I'm not really very interested in getting married, I've never taken the trouble to investigate.'

There was a pause. The Governor's cigar had gone out. He spent a moment or two getting it going again. When he spoke it seemed to Bond that the even tone had gained a spark of life, of interest. The Governor said: 'There was a man I knew once who must have had the same ideas as you. He fell in love with an air hostess and married her. Rather an interesting story, as a matter of fact. I suppose,' the Governor looked sideways at Bond and gave a short self-deprecatory laugh, 'you see quite a lot of the seamy side of life. This story may seem to you on the dull side. But would you care to hear it?'

'Very much.' Bond put enthusiasm into his voice. He doubted if the Governor's idea of what was seamy was the same as his own, but at least it would save him from making any more asinine conversation. Now to get away from this damnably cloying sofa. He said: 'Could I have some more brandy?' He got up, dashed an inch of brandy into his glass and, instead of going back to the sofa, pulled up a chair and sat down at an angle from the Governor on the other side of the drink tray.

The Governor examined the end of his cigar, took a quick pull and held the cigar upright so that the long ash would not fall off. He watched the ash warily throughout his story and spoke as if to the thin trickle of blue smoke that rose and quickly disappeared in the hot, moist air.

He said carefully: 'This man—I'll call him Masters, Philip Masters—was almost a contemporary of mine in the Service. I was a year ahead of him. He went to Fettes and took a schol-

arship for Oxford—the name of the college doesn't matter—
and then he applied for the Colonial Service. He wasn't a particularly clever chap, but he was hard working and capable
and the sort of man who makes a good solid impression on interview boards. They took him into the Service. His first post
was Nigeria. He did well in it. He liked the natives and he got
on well with them. He was a man of liberal ideas and while
he didn't actually fraternize, which,' the Governor smiled
sourly, 'would have got him into trouble with his superiors in
those days, he was lenient and humane towards the Nigerians.
It came as quite a surprise to them.' The Governor paused and
took a pull at his cigar. The ash was about to fall and he bent
carefully over towards the drink tray and let the ash hiss into
his coffee cup. He sat back and for the first time looked across
at Bond. He said: 'I daresay the affection this young man had
for the natives took the place of the affection young men of
that age in other walks of life have for the opposite sex. Un-
fortunately Philip Masters was a shy and rather uncouth
young man who had never had any kind of success in that direction. When he hadn't been working to pass his various
exams he had played hockey for his college and rowed in the
third eight. In the holidays he had stayed with an aunt in
Wales and climbed with the local mountaineering club. His
parents, by the way, had separated when he was at his public
school and, though he was an only child, had not bothered
with him once he was safe at Oxford with his scholarship and
a small allowance to see him through. So he had very little
time for girls and very little to recommend him to those he did
come across. His emotional life ran along the frustrated and
unhealthy lines that were part of our inheritance from our Vic-
torian grandfathers. Knowing how it was with him, I am there-
fore suggesting that his friendly relations with the coloured
people of Nigeria were what is known as a compensation
seized on by a basically warm and full-blooded nature that

had been starved of affection and now found it in their simple kindly natures.'

Bond interrupted the rather solemn narrative. 'The only trouble with beautiful Negresses is that they don't know anything about birth control. I hope he managed to stay out of that sort of trouble.'

The Governor held up his hand. His voice held an undertone of distaste for Bond's earthiness. 'No, no. You misunderstand me. I am not talking about sex. It would never have occurred to this young man to have relations with a coloured girl. In fact he was sadly ignorant of sexual matters. Not a rare thing even today among young people in England, but very common in those days, and the cause, as I expect you will agree, of many—very many—disastrous marriages and other tragedies.' Bond nodded. 'No. I am only explaining this young man at some length to show you that what was to come fell upon a frustrated young innocent with a warm but unawakened heart and body, and a social clumsiness which made him seek companionship and affection amongst the Negroes instead of in his own world He was, in short, a sensitive misfit, physically uninteresting, but in all other respects healthy and able and a perfectly adequate citizen.'

Bond took a sip of his brandy and stretched out his legs. He was enjoying the story. The Governor was telling it in a rather elderly narrative style which gave it a ring of truth.

The Governor continued: 'Young Masters's service in Nigeria coincided with the first Labour Government. If you remember, one of the first things they got down to was a reform of the foreign services. Nigeria got a new Governor with advanced views on the native problem who was surprised and pleased to find that he had a junior member of his staff who was already, in his modest sphere, putting something like the Governor's own views into practice. He encouraged Philip Masters, gave him duties which were above his rank, and in due course, when Masters was due for a move, he wrote such a glowing report that Masters jumped a grade and was transferred to Bermuda as Assistant Secretary to Government.'

The Governor looked through his cigar smoke at Bond. He said apologetically: 'I hope you aren't being too bored by all this. I shan't be long in coming to the point.'

'I'm very interested indeed. I think I've got a picture of the man. You must have known him well.'

The Governor hesitated. He said: 'I got to know him still better in Bermuda. I was just his senior and he worked directly under me. However, we haven't quite got to Bermuda yet. It was the early days of the air services to Africa and, for one reason or another, Philip Masters decided to fly home to London and so have a longer home leave than if he had taken ship from Freetown. He went by train to Nairobi and caught the weekly service of Imperial Airways—the forerunner of BOAC. He had never flown before and he was interested but slightly nervous when they took off, after the air hostess, whom he noticed was very pretty, had given him a sweet to suck and shown him how to fasten his seat-belt. When the plane had levelled out and he found that flying seemed a more peaceful business than he had expected, the hostess came back down the almost empty plane. She smiled at him. "You can undo the belt now." When Masters fumbled with the buckle she leant down and undid it for him. It was an intimate little gesture. Masters had never been so close to a woman of about his own age in his life. He blushed and felt an extraordinary confusion. He thanked her. She smiled rather saucily at his embarrassment and sat on the arm of the empty seat across the aisle and asked him where he had come from and where he was going. He told her. In his turn, he asked her about the plane and how fast they were flying and where they would stop, and so forth. He found her very easy to talk to and almost dazzlingly pretty to look at. He was surprised at her

easy way with him and her apparent interest in what he had
to say about Africa. She seemed to think he led a far more exciting and glamorous life than, to his mind, he did. She made
him feel important. When she went away to help the two
stewards prepare lunch, he sat and thought about her and
thrilled to his thoughts. When he tried to read he could not
focus on the page. He had to be looking up the plane to catch
a glimpse of her. Once she caught his gaze and gave him what
seemed to him a secret smile. We are the only young people
on the plane, it seemed to say. We understand each other.
We're interested in the same sort of things.

'Philip Masters gazed out of the window, seeing her in the
sea of white clouds below. In his mind's eye he examined her
minutely, marvelling at her perfection. She was small and
trim with a milk-and-roses complexion and fair hair tied in a
neat bun. (He particularly liked the bun. It suggested that she
wasn't "fast".) She had cherry red smiling lips and blue eyes
that sparkled with mischievous fun. Knowing Wales, he
guessed that she had Welsh blood in her, and this was con-
firmed by her name, Rhoda Llewellyn, which, when he went
to wash his hands before luncheon, he found printed at the
bottom of the crew list above the magazine rack beside the
lavatory door. He speculated deeply about her. She would be
near him now for nearly two days, but how could he get to see
her again? She must have hundreds of admirers. She might
even be married. Did she fly all the time? How many days off
did she get between trips? Would she laugh at him if he asked
her out to dinner and a theatre? Might she even complain to
the captain of the aircraft that one of the passengers was getting fresh? A sudden vision came to Masters of being turned
off the plane at Aden, a complaint to the Colonial Office, his
career ruined.

'Luncheon came, and reassurance. When she fitted the little
tray across his knees, her hair brushed his cheek. Masters felt

that he had been touched by a live electric wire. She showed him how to deal with the complicated little cellophane packages, how to get the plastic lid off the salad dressing. She told him that the sweet was particularly good—a rich layer cake. In short she made a fuss of him, and Masters couldn't remember when it had ever happened before, even when his mother had looked after him as a child.

'At the end of the trip, when the sweating Masters had screwed up his courage to ask her out to dinner, it was almost an anticlimax when she readily agreed. A month later she resigned from Imperial Airways and they were married. A month after that, Masters's leave was up and they took ship for Bermuda.'

Bond said: 'I fear the worst. She married him because his life sounded exciting and "grand". She liked the idea of being the belle of the tea parties at Government House. I suppose Masters had to murder her in the end?'

'No,' said the Governor mildly. 'But I daresay you're right about why she married him, that and being tired of the grind and danger of flying. Perhaps she really meant to make a go of it, and certainly when the young couple arrived and settled into their bungalow on the outskirts of Hamilton we were all favourably impressed by her vivacity and her pretty face and by the way she made herself pleasant to everyone. And, of course, Masters was a changed man. Life had become a fairytale for him. Looking back, it was almost pitiful to watch him try to spruce himself up so that he could live up to her. He took trouble about his clothes, put some dreadful brilliantine on his hair and even grew a military-type moustache, presumably because she thought it looked distinguished. At the end of the day, he would hurry back to the bungalow, and it was always Rhoda this and Rhoda that and when do you think Lady Burford—who was the Governor's wife—is going to ask Rhoda to lunch?

'But he worked hard and everyone liked the young couple, and things went along like a marriage bell for six months or so. Then, and now I'm only guessing, the occasional word began to drop like acid in the happy little bungalow. You can imagine the sort of thing: "Why doesn't the Colonial Secretary's wife ever take me out shopping with her? How long must we wait before we can give another cocktail party? You know we can't afford to have a baby. When are you due for promotion? It's awfully dull here all day with nothing to do. You'll have to get the dinner tonight. I simply can't be bothered. You have such an interesting time. It's all right for you . . ." and so on and so forth. And of course the cosseting quickly went by the board. Now it was Masters, and of course he was delighted to do it, who brought the air hostess breakfast in bed before he went off to work. It was Masters who tidied up the house when he came back in the evening and found cigarette ash and chocolate papers all over the place. It was Masters who had to give up smoking and his occasional drink to buy her new clothes so that she could live up to the other wives. Some of this showed, at any rate to me who knew Masters well, in the Secretariat. The preoccupied frown, the occasional enigmatic, over-solicitous telephone call in office hours, the ten minutes stolen at the end of the day so that he could take Rhoda to the cinema, and, of course, the occasional half joking questions about marriage in general: What do other wives do all day long? Do most women find it a bit hot out here? I suppose women (he almost added "God bless 'em") are much more easily upset than men. And so forth. The trouble, or at least most of it, was that Masters was besotted. She was his sun and his moon and if she was unhappy or restless it was all his fault. He cast about desperately for something that would occupy her and make her happy, and finally, of all things, he settled—or rather they settled together—on golf. Golf is very much the thing in Bermuda. There are several fine links—including the famous Mid-Ocean Club where all the quality play and get together at the club afterwards for gossip and drinks. It was just what she wanted—a smart occupation and high society. God knows how Masters saved up enough to join and buy her the clubs and the lessons and all the rest, but somehow he did it and it was a roaring success. She took to spending all day at the Mid-Ocean. She worked hard at her lessons and got a handicap and met people through the little competitions and the monthly medals, and in six months she was not only playing a respectable game but had become quite the darling of the men members. I wasn't surprised. I remember seeing her there from time to time, a delicious, sunburned little figure in the shortest of shorts with a white eyeshade with a green lining, and a trim compact swing that flattered her figure, and I can tell you,' the Governor twinkled briefly, 'she was the prettiest thing I've ever seen on a golf course. Of course the next step didn't take long. There was a mixed-foursome competition. She was partnered with the oldest Tattersall boy—they're the leading Hamilton merchants and more or less the ruling clique in Bermudan society. He was a young hellion—handsome as be damned, a beautiful swimmer and a scratch golfer, with an open MG and a speedboat and all the trimmings. You know the type. Got all the girls he wanted, and, if they didn't sleep with him pretty quickly, they didn't get the rides in the MG or the Chriscraft or the evenings in the local night clubs. The couple won the competition after a hard fight in the final and Philip Masters was in the fashionable crowd round the eighteenth green to cheer them home. That was the last time he cheered for many a long day, perhaps for all his life. Almost at once she started "going" with young Tattersall, and once started she went like the wind. And believe me, Mr Bond'—the Governor closed a fist and brought it softly down on the edge of the drinks table—'it was ghastly to see. She didn't make the smallest attempt to soften the blow or hide the affair in any way. She just took young Tattersall and hit Masters in the face with him, and went on hitting. She would come home at any hour of the night—she had insisted that Masters should move into the spare room, some pretext about it being too hot to sleep together—and if she ever tidied the house or cooked him a meal it was only makeshift and to keep up some kind of appearance. Of course, in a month, the whole thing was public property and poor Masters was wearing the biggest pair of horns that had ever been seen in the Colony. Lady Burford finally stepped in and gave Rhoda Masters a talking to—said she was ruining her husband's career and so forth. But the trouble was that Lady Burford found Masters a pretty dull dog, and having perhaps had one or two escapades in her own youth—she was still a handsome woman with a twinkle in her eye—she was probably a bit too lenient with the girl. Of course Masters himself, as he was to tell me later, went through the usual dreary sequence—remonstrance, bitter quarrel, furious rage, violence (he told me he damned nearly throttled her one night) and, finally, icy withdrawal and sullen misery.' The Governor paused.' I don't know if you've ever seen a heart being broken, Mr Bond, broken slowly and deliberately. Well, that's what I saw happening to Philip Masters, and it was a dreadful thing to watch. There he had been, a man with Paradise in his face, and, within a year of his arrival in Bermuda, Hell was written all over it. Of course I did my best, we all did in one way or another, but once it had happened, on that eighteenth green at the Mid-Ocean, there was really nothing to do but try and pick up the bits. But Masters was like a wounded dog. He just drew away from us into a corner and snarled when anyone tried to come near him. I even went to the length of writing him one or two letters. He later told me he had torn them up without reading them. One day, several of us got together and asked him to a stag party in my bungalow. We tried to get him drunk. We got him drunk all right. The next thing that happened was a crash from the bathroom. Masters had tried to cut his wrists with my razor. That broke our nerve and I was deputed to go and see the Governor about the whole business. The Governor knew about it, of course, but had hoped he wouldn't have to interfere. Now the question was whether Masters could even stay on in the Service. His work had gone to pieces. His wife was a public scandal. He was a broken man. Could we stick the bits together again? The Governor was a fine man. Once action had been forced on him, he was determined to make a last effort to stave off the almost inevitable report to Whitehall which would finally smash what remained of Masters. And Providence stepped in to lend a hand. The very next day after my interview with the Governor, there was a dispatch from the Colonial Office saying there was to be a meeting in Washington to delineate off-shore fishing rights, and that Bermuda and the Bahamas had been invited to send representatives of their Governments. The Governor sent for Masters, spoke to him like a Dutch uncle, told him that he was being sent to Washington and that he had better have his domestic affairs settled one way or the other in the next six months, and packed him off. Masters left in a week and sat in Washington talking fish for five months, and we all heaved a sigh of relief and cut Rhoda Masters whenever we could find an opportunity to do it.'

The Governor stopped speaking and it was silent in the big, brightly lit drawing-room. He took out a handkerchief and wiped it over his face. His memories had excited him and his eyes were bright in the flushed face. He got to his feet and poured a whisky and soda for Bond, and one for himself.

Bond said: 'What a mess. I suppose something like that was bound to happen sooner or later, but it was bad luck on Masters that it had to happen so soon. She must have been a hard-hearted little bitch. Did she show any signs of being sorry for what she'd done?'

The Governor had finished lighting a fresh cigar. He looked at the glowing tip and blew on it. He said: 'Oh no. She was having a wonderful time. She probably knew it wouldn't last for ever, but it was what she had dreamed about—what the readers of women's magazines dream about, and she was pretty typical of that sort of mentality. She had everything— the best catch on the island, love on the sands under the palm trees, gay times in the town and at the Mid-Ocean, fast drives in the car and the speedboat—all the trappings of cheap romance. And, to fall back on, a slave of a husband well out of the way, and a house to have a bath in and change her clothes and get some sleep. And she knew she could get Philip Masters back. He was so abject. There would be no difficulty. And then she could go round and apologize to everyone and turn on the charm again and everyone would forgive her. It would be all right. If it wasn't all right, there were plenty of other men in the world besides Philip Masters—and more attractive ones at that. Why, look at all the men at the golf club! She could have her pick of them at the drop of a hat. No, life was good, and if one was being a bit naughty it was after all only the way plenty of other people behaved. Look at the way the filmstars went on in Hollywood.

'Well, she was soon put to the test. Tattersall got a bit tired of her and, thanks to the Governor's wife, the Tattersall parents were making the hell of a fuss. That gave Tattersall a good excuse to get out of it all without too much of a scene. And it was summer and the island was flooded with pretty American girls. It was time for some fresh blood. So he chucked Rhoda Masters. Like that. Just told her they were through. That his parents had insisted or they would cut off his allowance. It was a fortnight before Philip Masters was due back from

Washington, and I will say she took it well. She was tough and
she had known it would have to come some time or other. She
didn't squeal. For that matter there was no one to squeal to.
She just went and told Lady Burford that she was sorry and
that she was now going to be a good wife to Philip Masters,
and she started on the house and cleaned it up and got everything shipshape ready for the big reconciliation scene. The ne-
cessity for bringing about this reconciliation was made clear
to her by the attitude of her former cronies at the Mid-Ocean.
She had suddenly become bad news there. You know how
these things can happen, even in an open-handed place like a
country club in the tropics. Now not only the Government
House set but also the Hamilton merchants clique frowned on
her. She was suddenly shoddy goods, used and discarded.
She tried to be the same gay little flirt, but it didn't work any
more. She got sharply snubbed once or twice and stopped
going. Now it was vital to get back to a secure base and start
slowly working her way up again. She stayed at home and set
to with a will, rehearsing over and over again the act she
would put on—the tears, the air hostess cosseting, the lengthy,
sincere excuses and explanations, the double bed.

'And then Philip Masters came home.'

The Governor paused and looked reflectively over at Bond.
He said: 'You're not married, but I think it's the same with all
relationships between a man and a woman. They can survive
anything so long as some kind of basic humanity exists between the two people. When all kindness has gone, when one
person obviously and sincerely doesn't care if the other is
alive or dead, then it's just no good. That particular insult to
the ego—worse, to the instinct of self-preservation—can never
be forgiven. I've noticed this in hundreds of marriages. I've
seen flagrant infidelities patched up, I've seen crimes and
even murder forgiven by the other party, let alone bankruptcy
and every other form of social crime. Incurable disease, blind-

ness, disaster—all these can be overcome. But never the death of common humanity in one of the partners. I've thought about this and I've invented a rather high-sounding title for this basic factor in human relations. I have called it the Law of the Quantum of Solace.

Bond said: 'That's a splendid name for it. It's certainly impressive enough. And of course I see what you mean. I should say you're absolutely right. Quantum of Solace—the amount of comfort. Yes, I suppose you could say that all love and friendship is based in the end on that. Human beings are very insecure. When the other person not only makes you feel insecure but actually seems to want to destroy you, it's obviously the end. The Quantum of Solace stands at zero. You've got to get away to save yourself. Did Masters see that?'

The Governor didn't answer the question. He said: 'Rhoda Masters should have been warned when her husband walked through the bungalow door. It wasn't so much what she saw on the surface—though the moustache had gone and Masters's hair was once again the untidy mop of their first meeting—it was the eyes and the mouth and the set of the chin. Rhoda Masters had put on her quietest frock. She had taken off most of her make-up and had arranged herself in a chair where the light from the window left her face in half shadow and illuminated the pages of a book on her lap. She had decided that, when he came through the door, she would look up from her book, docilely, submissively and wait for him to speak. Then she would get up and come quietly to him and stand in front of him with her head bowed. She would tell him all and let the tears come and he would take her in his arms and she would promise and promise. She had practised the scene many times until she was satisfied.

'She duly glanced up from her book. Masters quietly put down his suitcase and walked slowly over to the mantelpiece and stood looking vaguely down at her. His eyes were cold and impersonal and without interest. He put his hand in his inside pocket and took out a piece of paper. He said in the matter-of-fact voice of a house agent: "Here is a plan of the house. I have divided the house in two. Your rooms are the kitchen and your bedroom. Mine are this room and the spare bedroom. You may use the bathroom when I am not in it." He leant over and dropped the paper on the open pages of her book. "You are never to enter my rooms except when we have friends in." Rhoda Masters opened her mouth to speak. He held up his hand. "This is the last time I shall speak to you in private. If you speak to me, I shall not answer. If you wish to communicate, you may leave a note in the bathroom. I shall expect my meals to be prepared punctually and placed in the dining-room, which you may use when I have finished. I shall give you twenty pounds a month to cover the housekeeping, and this amount will be sent to you by my lawyers on the first of each month. My lawyers are preparing the divorce papers. I am divorcing you, and you will not fight the action because you cannot. A private detective has provided full evidence against you. The action will take place in one year from now when my time in Bermuda is up. In the meantime, in public, we shall behave as a normal married couple."

'Masters put his hands in his pockets and looked politely down at her. By this time tears were pouring down her face. She looked terrified—as if someone had hit her. Masters said indifferently: "Is there anything else you'd like to know? If not, you had better collect your belongings from here and move into the kitchen." He looked at his watch. "I would like dinner every evening at eight. It is now seven-thirty."'

The Governor paused and sipped his whisky. He said: 'I've put all this together from the little that Masters told me and from fuller details Rhoda Masters gave to Lady Burford. Apparently Rhoda Masters tried every way to shake him—arguments, pleadings, hysterics. He was unmoved. She simply couldn't reach him. It was as if he had gone away and had sent someone else to the house to represent him at this extraordinary interview. And in the end she had to agree. She had no money. She couldn't possibly afford the passage to England. To have a bed and food she had to do what he told her. And so it was. For a year they lived like that, polite to each other in public, but utterly silent and separate when they were alone. Of course, we were all astonished by the change. Neither of them told anyone of the arrangement. She would have been ashamed to do so and there was no reason why Masters should. He seemed to us a bit more withdrawn than before, but his work was first-class and everyone heaved a sigh of relief and agreed that by some miracle the marriage had been saved. Both of them gained great credit from the fact, and they became a popular couple with everything forgiven and forgotten.

'The year passed and it was time for Masters to go. He announced that Rhoda would stay behind to close the house, and they went through the usual round of farewell parties. We were a bit surprised that she didn't come to see him off in the ship, but he said she wasn't feeling well. So that was that until, in a couple of weeks, news of the divorce case began leaking back from England. Then Rhoda Masters turned up at Government House and had a long interview with Lady Burford, and gradually the whole story, including its really terrible next chapter, leaked out '

The Governor swallowed the last of his whisky. The ice made a hollow rattle as he put the glass softly down. He said: 'Apparently on the day before Masters left he found a note from his wife in the bathroom. It said that she simply must see him for one last talk before he left her for ever. There had been notes like this before and Masters had always torn them up and left the bits on the shelf above the basin. This time he scribbled a note giving her an appointment in the sitting-room

at six o'clock that evening. When the time arrived, Rhoda
Masters came meekly in from the kitchen. She had long since
given up making emotional scenes or trying to throw herself
on his mercy. Now she just quietly stood and said that she had
only ten pounds left from that month's housekeeping money
and nothing else in the world. When he left she would be destitute.

' "You have the jewels I gave you, and the fur cape."

' "I'd be lucky if I got fifty pounds for them."

' "You'll have to get some work."

' "It'll take time to find something. I've got to live somewhere. I have to be out of the house in a fortnight. Won't you
give me anything at all? I shall starve."

'Masters looked at her dispassionately. "You're pretty.
You'll never starve."

' "You must help me, Philip. You must. It won't help your
career having me begging at Government House."

'Nothing in the house belonged to them except a few odds
and ends. They had taken it furnished. The owner had come
the week before and agreed the inventory. There only remained their car, a Morris that Masters had bought second
hand, and a radiogramophone he had bought as a last resort to
try and keep his wife amused before she took up golf.

'Philip Masters looked at her for the last time. He was never
to see her again. He said: "All right. You can have the car and
the radiogram. Now that's all. I've got to pack. Goodbye." And
he walked out of the door and up to his room.'

The Governor looked across at Bond. 'At least one last little
gesture. Yes?' The Governor smiled grimly. 'When he had
gone and Rhoda Masters was left alone, she took the car and
her engagement ring and her few trinkets and the fox fur tip-
pet and went into Hamilton and drove round the pawn-
brokers. In the end she collected forty pounds for the
jewellery and seven pounds for the bit of fur. Then she went

to the car dealers whose nameplate was on the dashboard of the car and asked to see the manager. When she asked how much he would give her for the Morris he thought she was pulling his leg. "But, madam, Mr Masters bought the car by hire purchase and he's very badly behind on his payments. Surely he told you that we had to send him a solicitor's letter about it only a week ago. We heard he was leaving. He wrote back that you would be coming in to make the necessary arrangements. Let me see"—he reached for a file and leafed through it. "Yes, there's exactly two hundred pounds owing on the car."

'Well, of course, Rhoda Masters burst into tears and in the end the manager agreed to take back the car, although it wasn't worth two hundred pounds by then, but he insisted that she should leave it with him then and there, petrol in the tank and all. Rhoda Masters could only accept and be grateful not to be sued, and she walked out of the garage and along the hot street and already she knew what she was going to find when she got to the radio shop. And she was right. It was the same story, only this time she had to pay ten pounds to persuade the man to take back the radiogram. She got a lift back to within walking distance of the bungalow and went and threw herself down on the bed and cried for the rest of the day. She had already been a beaten woman. Now Philip Masters had kicked her when she was down.'

The Governor paused. 'Pretty extraordinary, really. A man like Masters, kindly, sensitive, who wouldn't normally hurt a fly. And here he was performing one of the cruellest actions I can recall in all my experience. It was my law operating.' The Governor smiled thinly. 'Whatever her sins, if she had given him that Quantum of Solace he could never have behaved to her as he did. As it was, she had awakened in him a bestial cruelty—a cruelty that perhaps lies deeply hidden in all of us and that only a threat to our existence can bring to the surface.

Masters wanted to make the girl suffer, not as much as he had suffered because that was impossible, but as much as he could possibly contrive. And that false gesture with the motor car and the radiogramophone was a fiendishly brilliant bit of delayed action to remind her, even when he was gone, how much he hated her, how much he wanted still to hurt her.'

Bond said: 'It must have been a shattering experience. It's extraordinary how much people can hurt each other. I'm beginning to feel rather sorry for the girl. What happened to her in the end—and to him, for the matter of that?'

The Governor got to his feet and looked at his watch. 'Good heavens, it's nearly midnight. And I've been keeping the staff up all this time,' he smiled, 'as well as you.' He walked across to the fireplace and rang a bell. A Negro butler appeared. The Governor apologized for keeping him up and told him to lock up and turn the light out. Bond was on his feet. The Governor turned to him. 'Come along and I'll tell you the rest. I'll walk through the garden with you and see that the sentry lets you out.'

They walked slowly through the long rooms and down the broad steps to the garden. It was a beautiful night under a full moon that raced over their heads through the thin high clouds.

The Governor said: 'Masters went on in the Service, but somehow he never lived up to his good start. After the Bermuda business something seemed to go out of him. Part of him had been killed by the experience. He was a maimed man. Mostly her fault, of course, but I guess that what he did to her lived on with him and perhaps haunted him. He was good at his work, but he had somehow lost the human touch and he gradually dried up. Of course he never married again and in the end he got shunted off into the ground nuts scheme, and when that was a failure he retired and went to live in Nigeria—back to the only people in the world who had shown him any kindness—back to where it had all started from. Bit tragic, really, when I remember what he was like when we were young.'

'And the girl?'

'Oh, she went through a pretty bad time. We handed round the hat for her and she pottered in and out of various jobs that were more or less charity. She tried to go back to being an air hostess, but the way she had broken her contract with Imperial Airways put her out of the running for that. There weren't so many airlines in those days and there was no shortage of applicants for the few hostess jobs that were going. The Burfords got transferred to Jamaica later in that same year and that removed her main prop. As I said, Lady Burford had always had a soft spot for her. Rhoda Masters was pretty nearly destitute. She still had her looks and various men had kept her for a while; but you can't make the rounds for very long in a small place like Bermuda, and she was very near to becoming a harlot and getting into trouble with the police when Providence again stepped in and decided she had been punished enough. A letter came from Lady Burford enclosing her fare to Jamaica and saying she had got her a job as receptionist at the Blue Hills Hotel, one of the best of the Kingston hotels. So she left, and I expect— I'd been transferred to Rhodesia by then—that Bermuda was heartily relieved to see the last of her.'

The Governor and Bond had come to the wide entrance gates to the grounds of Government House. Beyond them shone, white and black and pink under the moon, the huddle of narrow streets and pretty clapboard houses with gingerbread gables and balconies that is Nassau. With a terrific clatter the sentry came to attention and presented arms. The Governor raised a hand: 'All right. Stand at ease.' Again the clockwork sentry rattled briefly into life and there was silence.

The Governor said: 'And that's the end of the story except for one final quirk of fate. One day a Canadian millionaire turned up at the Blue Hills Hotel and stayed for the winter. At the end of the time he took Rhoda Masters back to Canada and married her. She's lived in clover ever since.'

'Good heavens. That was a stroke of luck. Hardly deserved it.'

'I suppose not. One can't tell. Life's a devious business. Perhaps, for all the harm she'd done to Masters, Fate decided that she had paid back enough. Perhaps Masters's father and mother were the true guilty people. They turned Masters into an accident-prone man. Inevitably he was involved in the emotional crash that was due to him and that they had conditioned him for. Fate had chosen Rhoda for its instrument. Now Fate reimbursed her for her services. Difficult to judge these things. Anyway, she made her Canadian very happy. I thought they both seemed happy tonight.'

Bond laughed. Suddenly the violent dramatics of his own life seemed very hollow. The affair of the Castro rebels and the burned out yachts was the stuff of an adventure-strip in a cheap newspaper. He had sat next to a dull woman at a dull dinner party and a chance remark had opened for him the book of real violence—of the Comédie Humaine where human passions are raw and real, where Fate plays a more authentic game than any Secret Service conspiracy devised by Governments.

Bond faced the Governor and held out his hand. He said: 'Thank you for the story. And I owe you an apology. I found Mrs Harvey Miller a bore. Thanks to you I shall never forget her. I must pay more attention to people. You've taught me a lesson.'

They shook hands. The Governor smiled. 'I'm glad the story interested you. I was afraid you might be bored. You lead a very exciting life. To tell you the truth, I was at my wit's end to know what we could talk about after dinner. Life in the Colonial Service is very humdrum.'

They said goodnight. Bond walked off down the quiet street towards the harbour and the British Colonial Hotel. He reflected on the conference he would be having in the morning with the Coast Guard and the FBI in Miami. The prospect, which had previously interested, even excited him, was now edged with boredom and futility.

'In this pizniss is much risico.'

The words came softly through the thick brown moustache. The hard black eyes moved slowly over Bond's face and down to Bond's hands which were carefully shredding a paper match on which was printed *Albergo Colomba d'Oro*.

James Bond felt the inspection. The same surreptitious examination had been going on since he had met the man two hours before at the rendezvous in the Excelsior bar. Bond had been told to look for a man with a heavy moustache who would be sitting by himself drinking an Alexandra. Bond had been amused by this secret recognition signal. The creamy, feminine drink was so much cleverer than the folded newspaper, the flower in the buttonhole, the yellow gloves that were the hoary, slipshod call-signs between agents. It had also the great merit of being able to operate alone, without its owner. And Kristatos had started off with a little test. When Bond had come into the bar and looked round there had been perhaps twenty people in the room. None of them had a moustache. But on a corner table at the far side of the tall, discreet room, flanked by a saucer of olives and another of cashew nuts, stood the tall-stemmed glass of cream and vodka. Bond went straight over to the table, pulled out a chair and sat down.

The waiter came. 'Good evening, sir. Signor Kristatos is at the telephone.'

Bond nodded. 'A Negroni. With Gordon's, please.'

The waiter walked back to the bar. 'Negroni. Uno. Gordon's.'

'I am so sorry.' The big hairy hand picked up the small chair as if it had been as light as a matchbox and swept it under the heavy hips. 'I had to have a word with Alfredo.'

There had been no handshake. These were old acquaintances. In the same line of business, probably. Something like import and export. The younger one looked American. No. Not with those clothes. English.

Bond returned the fast serve. 'How's his little boy?'

The black eyes of Signor Kristatos narrowed. Yes, they had said this man was a professional. He spread his hands. 'Much the same. What can you expect?'

'Polio is a terrible thing.

The Negroni came. The two men sat back comfortably, each one satisfied that he had to do with a man in the same league. This was rare in 'The Game'. So many times, before one had even started on a tandem assignment like this, one had lost confidence in the outcome. There was so often, at least in Bond's imagination, a faint smell of burning in the air at such a rendezvous. He knew it for the sign that the fringe of his cover had already started to smoulder. In due course the smouldering fabric would burst into flames and he would be *brûlé*. Then the game would be up and he would have to decide whether to pull out or wait and get shot at by someone. But at this meeting there had been no fumbling.

Later that evening, at the little restaurant off the Piazza di Spagna called the Colomba d'Oro, Bond was amused to find that he was still on probation. Kristatos was still watching and weighing him, wondering if he could be trusted. This remark about the risky business was as near as Kristatos had so far got to admitting that there existed any business between the two of them. Bond was encouraged. He had not really believed in

Kristatos. But surely all these precautions could only mean
that M's intuition had paid off—that Kristatos knew something big.

Bond dropped the last shred of match into the ashtray. He
said mildly: 'I was once taught that any business that pays
more than ten per cent or is conducted after nine o'clock at
night is a dangerous business. The business which brings us
together pays up to one thousand per cent and is conducted
almost exclusively at night. On both counts it is obviously a
risky business.' Bond lowered his voice. 'Funds are available.
Dollars, Swiss francs, Venezuelan bolivars—anything convenient.'

'That makes me glad. I have already too much lire.' Signor
Kristatos picked up the folio menu. 'But let us feed on something. One should not decide important pizniss on a hollow
stomach.'

A week earlier M had sent for Bond. M was in a bad temper.
'Got anything on, 007?'

'Only paper work, sir.'

'What do you mean, only paper work?' M jerked his pipe
towards his loaded in-tray. 'Who hasn't got paper work?'

'I meant nothing active, sir.'

'Well, say so.' M picked up a bundle of dark red files tied together with tape and slid them so sharply across the desk that
Bond had to catch them. 'And here's some more paper work.
Scotland Yard stuff mostly—their narcotics people. Wads
from the Home Office and the Ministry of Health, and some
nice thick reports from the International Opium Control people in Geneva. Take it away and read it. You'll need today and
most of tonight. Tomorrow you fly to Rome and get after the
big men. Is that clear?'

Bond said that it was. The state of M's temper was also explained. There was nothing that made him more angry than

having to divert his staff from their primary duty. This duty
was espionage, and when necessary sabotage and subversion.
Anything else was a misuse of the Service and of Secret Funds
which, God knows, were meagre enough.

'Any questions?' M's jaw stuck out like the prow of a ship.
The jaw seemed to tell Bond to pick up the files and get the
hell out of the office and let M move on to something important.

Bond knew that a part of all this—if only a small part—was
an act. M had certain bees in his bonnet. They were famous in
the Service, and M knew they were. But that did not mean
that he would allow them to stop buzzing. There were queen
bees, like the misuse of the Service, and the search for true as
distinct from wishful intelligence, and there were worker
bees. These included such idiosyncrasies as not employing
men with beards, or those who were completely bilingual, in-
stantly dismissing men who tried to bring pressure to bear on
him through family relationships with members of the Cabi-
net, mistrusting men or women who were too 'dressy', and
those who called him 'sir' off-duty; and having an exaggerated
faith in Scotsmen. But M was ironically conscious of his ob-
sessions, as, thought Bond, a Churchill or a Montgomery were
about theirs. He never minded his bluff, as it partly was, being
called on any of them. Moreover, he would never have
dreamed of sending Bond out on an assignment without
proper briefing.

Bond knew all this. He said mildly: 'Two things, sir. Why
are we taking this thing on, and what lead, if any, have Station
I got towards the people involved in it?'

M gave Bond a hard, sour look. He swivelled his chair sideways so that he could watch the high, scudding October
clouds through the broad window. He reached out for his
pipe, blew through it sharply, and then, as if this action had
let off the small head of steam, replaced it gently on the desk.

When he spoke, his voice was patient, reasonable. 'As you can imagine, 007, I do not wish the Service to become involved in this drug business. Earlier this year I had to take you off other duties for a fortnight so that you could go to Mexico and chase off that Mexican grower. You nearly got yourself killed. I sent you as a favour to the Special Branch. When they asked for you again to tackle this Italian gang I refused. Ronnie Vallance went behind my back to the Home Office and the Ministry of Health. The Ministers pressed me. I said that you were needed here and that I had no one else to spare. Then the two Ministers went to the PM.' M paused. 'And that was that. I must say the PM was very persuasive. Took the line that heroin, in the quantities that have been coming in, is an instrument of psychological warfare—that it saps a country's strength. He said he wouldn't be surprised to find that this wasn't just a gang of Italians out to make big money—that subversion and not money was at the back of it.' M smiled sourly. 'I expect Ronnie Vallance thought up that line of argument. Apparently his narcotics people have been having the devil of a time with the traffic—trying to stop it getting a hold on the teenagers as it has in America. Seems the dance halls and the amusement arcades are full of pedlars. Vallance's Ghost Squad have managed to penetrate back up the line to one of the middle-men, and there's no doubt it's all coming from Italy, hidden in Italian tourists' cars. Vallance has done what he can through the Italian police and Interpol, and got nowhere. They get so far back up the pipeline, arrest a few little people, and then, when they seem to be getting near the centre, there's a blank wall. The inner ring of distributors are too frightened or too well paid.'

Bond interrupted. 'Perhaps there's protection somewhere, sir. That Montesi business didn't look so good.'

M shrugged impatiently. 'Maybe, maybe. And you'll have to watch out for that too, but my impression is that the Montesi case resulted in a pretty extensive clean-up. Anyway, when the PM gave me the order to get on with it, it occurred to me to have a talk with Washington. CIA were very helpful. You know the Narcotics Bureau have a team in Italy. Have had ever since the War. They're nothing to do with CIA—run by the American Treasury Department, of all people. The American Treasury control a so-called Secret Service that looks after drug smuggling and counterfeiting. Pretty crazy arrangement. Often wonder what the FBI must think of it. However,' M slowly swivelled his chair away from the window. He linked his hands behind his head and leaned back, looking across the desk at Bond. 'The point is that the CIA Rome Station works pretty closely with this little narcotics team. Has to, to prevent crossed lines and so on. And CIA—Alan Dulles himself, as a matter of fact—gave me the name of the top narcotics agent used by the Bureau. Apparently he's a double. Does a little smuggling as cover. Chap called Kristatos. Dulles said that of course he couldn't involve his people in any way and he was pretty certain the Treasury Department wouldn't welcome their Rome Bureau playing too closely with us. But he said that, if I wished, he would get word to this Kristatos that one of our, er, best men would like to make contact with a view to doing business. I said I would much appreciate that, and yesterday I got word that the rendezvous is fixed for the day after tomorrow.' M gestured towards the files in front of Bond. 'You'll find all the details in there.'

There was a brief silence in the room. Bond was thinking that the whole affair sounded unpleasant, probably dangerous and certainly dirty. With the last quality in mind, Bond got to his feet and picked up the files. 'All right, sir. It looks like money. How much will we pay for the traffic to stop?'

M let his chair tip forward. He put his hands flat down on the desk, side by side. He said roughly: 'A hundred thousand pounds. In any currency. That's the PM's figure. But I don't

want you to get hurt. Certainly not picking other people's
coals out of the fire. So you can go up to another hundred
thousand if there's bad trouble. Drugs are the biggest and
tightest ring in crime.' M reached for his in-basket and took
out a file of signals. Without looking up he said: 'Look after
yourself.'

Signor Kristatos picked up the menu. He said: 'I do not beat
about bushes, Mr Bond. How much?'

'Fifty thousand pounds for one hundred per cent results.'

Kristatos said indifferently: 'Yes. Those are important
funds. I shall have melon with prosciutto ham and a chocolate
ice-cream. I do not eat greatly at night. These people have
their own Chianti. I commend it.'

The waiter came and there was a brisk rattle of Italian. Bond
ordered Tagliatelli Verdi with a Genoese sauce which Kristatos said was improbably concocted of basil, garlic and fir
cones.

When the waiter had gone, Kristatos sat and chewed
silently on a wooden toothpick. His face gradually became
dark and glum as if bad weather had come to his mind. The
black, hard eyes that glanced restlessly at everything in the
restaurant except Bond, glittered. Bond guessed that Kristatos
was wondering whether or not to betray somebody. Bond said
encouragingly: 'In certain circumstances, there might be
more.'

Kristatos seemed to make up his mind. He said: 'So?' He
pushed back his chair and got up. 'Forgive me. I must visit the
toiletta.' He turned and walked swiftly towards the back of the
restaurant.

Bond was suddenly hungry and thirsty. He poured out a
large glass of Chianti and swallowed half of it. He broke a roll
and began eating, smothering each mouthful with deep yellow butter. He wondered why rolls and butter are delicious

only in France and Italy. There was nothing else on his mind.
It was just a question of waiting. He had confidence in Kristatos. He was a big, solid man who was trusted by the Americans. He was probably making some telephone call that would
be decisive. Bond felt in good spirits. He watched the passers-
by through the plate-glass window. A man selling one of the
Party papers went by on a bicycle. Flying from the basket in
front of the handlebars was a pennant. In red on white it said:
PROGRESSO?—SI!—AVVENTURI?—NO! Bond smiled. That was
how it was. Let it so remain for the rest of the assignment.

On the far side of the square, rather plain room, at the corner
table by the *caisse*, the plump fair-haired girl with the dra-
matic mouth said to the jovial good-living man with the thick
rope of spaghetti joining his face to the plate: 'He has a rather
cruel smile. But he is very handsome. Spies aren't usually so
good-looking. Are you sure you are right, mein Täubchen?'

The man's teeth cut through the rope. He wiped his mouth
on a napkin already streaked with tomato sauce, belched
sonorously and said: 'Santos is never wrong about these
things. He has a nose for spies. That is why I chose him as the
permanent tail for that bastard Kristatos. And who else but a
spy would think of spending an evening with the pig? But we
will make sure.' The man took out of his pocket one of those
cheap tin snappers that are sometimes given out, with paper
hats and whistles, on carnival nights. It gave one sharp click.
The maître d'hôtel on the far side of the room stopped whatever he was doing and hurried over.

'Si, padrone.'

The man beckoned. The maître d'hôtel went over and re-
ceived the whispered instructions. He nodded briefly, walked
over to a door near the kitchens marked UFFICIO, and went in
and closed the door behind him.

Phase by phase, in a series of minute moves, an exercise

that had long been perfected was then smoothly put into effect. The man near the *caisse* munched his spaghetti and critically observed each step in the operation as if it had been a fast game of chess.

The maître d'hôtel came out of the door marked UFFICIO, hurried across the restaurant and said loudly to his No. 2: 'An extra table for four. Immediately.' The No. 2 gave him a direct look and nodded. He followed the maître d'hôtel over to a space adjoining Bond's table, clicked his fingers for help, borrowed a chair from one table, a chair from another table and, with a bow and an apology, the spare chair from Bond's table. The fourth chair was being carried over from the direction of the door marked UFFICIO by the maître d'hôtel. He placed it square with the others, a table was lowered into the middle and glass and cutlery were deftly laid. The maître d'hôtel frowned. 'But you have laid a table for four. I said three—for three people.' He casually took the chair he had himself brought to the table and switched it to Bond's table. He gave a wave of the hand to dismiss his helpers and everyone dispersed about their business.

The innocent little flurry of restaurant movement had taken about a minute. An innocuous trio of Italians came into the restaurant. The maître d'hôtel greeted them personally and bowed them to the new table, and the gambit was completed.

Bond had hardly been conscious of it. Kristatos returned from whatever business he had been about, their food came and they got on with the meal.

While they ate they talked about nothing—the election chances in Italy, the latest Alfa Romeo, Italian shoes compared with English. Kristatos talked well. He seemed to know the inside story of everything. He gave information so casually that it did not sound like bluff. He spoke his own kind of English with an occasional phrase borrowed from other languages. It made a lively mixture. Bond was interested and amused. Kristatos was a tough insider—a useful man. Bond was not surprised that the American Intelligence people found him good value.

Coffee came, Kristatos lit a thin black cigar and talked through it, the cigar jumping up and down between the thin straight lips. He put both hands flat on the table in front of him. He looked at the tablecloth between them and said softly: 'This pizniss. I will play with you. To now I have only played with the Americans. I have not told them what I am about to tell you. There was no requirement. This machina does not operate with America. These things are closely regulated. This machina operates only with England. Yes? Capito?'

'I understand. Everyone has his own territory. It's the usual way in these things.'

'Exact. Now, before I give you the informations, like good commercials we make the terms. Yes?'

'Of course.'

Signor Kristatos examined the tablecloth more closely. 'I wish for ten thousand dollars American, in paper of small sizes, by tomorrow lunchtime. When you have destroyed the machina I wish for a further twenty thousand.' Signor Kristatos briefly raised his eyes and surveyed Bond's face. 'I am not greedy. I do not take all your funds, isn't it?'

'The price is satisfactory.'

'Bueno. Second term. There is no telling where you get these informations from. Even if you are beaten.'

'Fair enough.'

'Third term. The head of this machina is a bad man.' Signor Kristatos paused and looked up. The black eyes held a red glint. The clenched dry lips pulled away from the cigar to let the words out. 'He is to be destrutto—killed.'

Bond sat back. He gazed quizzically at the other man who now leaned slightly forward over the table, waiting. So the wheels had now shown within the wheels! This was a private

vendetta of some sort. Kristatos wanted to get himself a gunman. And he was not paying the gunman, the gunman was
paying him for the privilege of disposing of an enemy. Not
bad! The fixer was certainly working on a big fix this time—
using the Secret Service to pay off his private scores. Bond
said softly: 'Why?'

Signor Kristatos said indifferently: 'No questions catch no
lies.'

Bond drank down his coffee. It was the usual story of big
syndicate crime. You never saw more than the tip of the ice-
berg. But what did that matter to him? He had been sent to do
one specific job. If his success benefited others, nobody, least
of all M, could care less. Bond had been told to destroy the
machine. If this unnamed man was the machine, it would be
merely carrying out orders to destroy the man. Bond said: 'I
cannot promise that. You must see that. All I can say is that if
the man tries to destroy me, I will destroy him.'

Signor Kristatos took a toothpick out of the holder, stripped
off the paper and set about cleaning his fingernails. When he
had finished one hand he looked up. He said: 'I do not often
gamble on incertitudes. This time I will do so because it is you
who are paying me, and not me you. Is all right? So now I will
give you the informations. Then you are alone—solo. Tomorrow night I fly to Karachi. I have important pizniss there. I can
only give you the informations. After that you run with the
ball and—' he threw the dirty toothpick down on the table—
'Che sera, sera.'

'All right.'

Signor Kristatos edged his chair nearer to Bond. He spoke
softly and quickly. He gave specimen dates and names to document his narrative. He never hesitated for a fact and he did
not waste time on irrelevant detail. It was a short story and a
pithy one. There were two thousand American gangsters in
the country—Italian-Americans who had been convicted and

expelled from the United States. These men were in a bad way. They were on the blackest of all police lists and, because of their records, their own people were wary of employing them. A hundred of the toughest among them had pooled their funds and small groups from this elite had moved to Beirut, Istanbul, Tangier and Macao—the great smuggling centres of the world. A further large section acted as couriers, and the bosses had acquired, through nominees, a small and respectable pharmaceutical business in Milan. To this centre the outlying groups smuggled opium and its derivatives. They used small craft across the Mediterranean, a group of stewards in an Italian charter airline and, as a regular weekly source of supply, the through carriage of the Orient Express in which whole sections of bogus upholstery were fitted by bribed members of the train cleaners in Istanbul. The Milan firm—Pharmacia Colomba SA—acted as a clearing-house and as a convenient centre for breaking down the raw opium into heroin. Thence the couriers using innocent motor cars of various makes, ran a delivery service to the middlemen in England.

Bond interrupted. 'Our Customs are pretty good at spotting that sort of traffic. There aren't many hiding-places in a car they don't know about. Where do these men carry the stuff?'

'Always in the spare wheel. You can carry twenty thousand pounds worth of heroin in one spare wheel.'

'Don't they ever get caught—either bringing the stuff in to Milan or taking it on?'

'Certainly. Many times. But these are well-trained men. And they are tough. They never talk. If they are convicted, they receive ten thousand dollars for each year spent in prison. If they have families, they are cared for. And when all goes well they make good money. It is a cooperative. Each man receives his *tranche* of the *brutto*. Only the chief gets a special *tranche*.'

'All right. Well, who is this man?'

Signor Kristatos put his hand up to the cheroot in his mouth. He kept the hand there and spoke softly from behind it. 'Is a man they call "The Dove", Enrico Colombo. Is the padrone of this restaurant. That is why I bring you here, so that you may see him. Is the fat man who sits with a blonde woman. At the table by the cassa. She is from Vienna. Her name is Lisl Baum. A luxus whore.'

Bond said reflectively: 'She is, is she?' He did not need to look. He had noticed the girl, as soon as he had sat down at the table. Every man in the restaurant would have noticed her. She had the gay, bold, forthcoming looks the Viennese are supposed to have and seldom do. There was a vivacity and a charm about her that lit up her corner of the room. She had the wildest possible urchin cut in ash blonde, a pert nose, a wide laughing mouth and a black ribbon round her throat. James Bond knew that her eyes had been on him at intervals throughout the evening. Her companion had seemed just the type of rich, cheerful, good-living man she would be glad to have as her lover for a while. He would give her a good time. He would be generous. There would be no regrets on either side. On the whole, Bond had vaguely approved of him. He liked cheerful, expansive people with a zest for life. Since he, Bond, could not have the girl, it was at least something that she was in good hands. But now? Bond glanced across the room. The couple were laughing about something. The man patted her cheek and got up and went to the door marked UF-FICIO and went through and shut the door. So this was the man who ran the great pipeline into England. The man with M's price of a hundred thousand pounds on his head. The man Kristatos wanted Bond to kill. Well, he had better get on with the job. Bond stared rudely across the room at the girl. When she lifted her head and looked at him, he smiled at her. Her eyes swept past him, but there was a half smile, as if for her-

self, on her lips, and when she took a cigarette out of her case
and lit it and blew the smoke straight up towards the ceiling
there was an offering of the throat and the profile that Bond
knew were for him.

It was nearing the time for the after-cinema trade. The
maître d'hôtel was supervising the clearing of the unoccupied
tables and the setting up of new ones. There was the usual
bustle and slapping of napkins across chair-seats and tinkle of
glass and cutlery being laid. Vaguely Bond noticed the spare
chair at his table being whisked away to help build up a
nearby table for six. He began asking Kristatos specific
questions—the personal habits of Enrico Colombo, where he
lived, the address of his firm in Milan, what other business interests he had. He did not notice the casual progress of the
spare chair from its fresh table to another, and then to another,
and finally through the door marked UFFICIO. There was no
reason why he should.

When the chair was brought into his office, Enrico Colombo
waved the maître d'hôtel away and locked the door behind
him. Then he went to the chair and lifted off the squab cush-
ion and put it on his desk. He unzipped one side of the cush-
ion and withdrew a Grundig tape-recorder, stopped the
machine, ran the tape back, took it off the recorder and put it
on a playback and adjusted the speed and volume. Then he
sat down at his desk and lit a cigarette and listened, occasionally making further adjustments and occasionally repeat-
ing passages. At the end, when Bond's tinny voice said 'She
is, is she?' and there was a long silence interspersed with
background noises from the restaurant, Enrico Colombo
switched off the machine and sat looking at it. He looked at it
for a full minute. His face showed nothing but acute concentration on his thoughts. Then he looked away from the machine and into nothing and said softly, out loud: 'Son-a-beech.'

He got slowly to his feet and went to the door and unlocked it. He looked back once more at the Grundig, said 'Son-a-beech' again with more emphasis and went out and back to his table.

Enrico Colombo spoke swiftly and urgently to the girl. She nodded and glanced across the room at Bond. He and Kristatos were getting up from the table. She said to Colombo in a low, angry voice: 'You are a disgusting man. Everybody said so and warned me against you. They were right. Just because you give me dinner in your lousy restaurant you think you have the right to insult me with your filthy propositions'—the girl's voice had got louder. Now she had snatched up her handbag and had got to her feet. She stood beside the table directly in the line of Bond's approach on his way to the exit.

Enrico Colombo's face was black with rage. Now he, too, was on his feet. 'You goddam Austrian beech—'

'Don't dare insult my country, you Italian toad.' She reached for a half-full glass of wine and hurled it accurately in the man's face. When he came at her it was easy for her to back the few steps into Bond who was standing with Kristatos politely waiting to get by.

Enrico Colombo stood panting, wiping the wine off his face with a napkin. He said furiously to the girl: 'Don't ever show your face inside my restaurant again.' He made the gesture of spitting on the floor between them, turned and strode off through the door marked UFFICIO.

The maître d'hôtel had hurried up. Everyone in the restaurant had stopped eating. Bond took the girl by the elbow. 'May I help you find a taxi?'

She jerked herself free. She said, still angry: 'All men are pigs.' She remembered her manners. She said stiffly: 'You are very kind.' She moved haughtily towards the door with the men in her wake.

There was a buzz in the restaurant and a renewed clatter of knives and forks. Everyone was delighted with the scene. The maître d'hôtel, looking solemn, held open the door. He said to Bond: 'I apologize, Monsieur. And you are very kind to be of assistance.' A cruising taxi slowed. He beckoned it to the pavement and held open the door.

The girl got in. Bond firmly followed and closed the door. He said to Kristatos through the window: 'I'll telephone you in the morning. All right?' Without waiting for the man's reply he sat back in the seat. The girl had drawn herself away into the farthest corner. Bond said: 'Where shall I tell him?'

'Hotel Ambassadori.'

They drove a short way in silence. Bond said: 'Would you like to go somewhere first for a drink?'

'No thank you.' She hesitated. 'You are very kind, but tonight I am tired.'

'Perhaps another night.'

'Perhaps, but I go to Venice tomorrow.'

'I shall also be there. Will you have dinner with me tomorrow night?'

The girl smiled. She said: 'I thought Englishmen were supposed to be shy. You are English, aren't you? What is your name? What do you do?'

'Yes, I'm English—My name's Bond—James Bond. I write books—adventure stories. I'm writing one now about drug smuggling. It's set in Rome and Venice. The trouble is that I don't know enough about the trade. I am going round picking up stories about it. Do you know any?'

'So that is why you were having dinner with that Kristatos. I know of him. He has a bad reputation. No. I don't know any stories. I only know what everybody knows.'

Bond said enthusiastically 'But that's exactly what I want. When I said "stories" I didn't mean fiction. I meant the sort of high-level gossip that's probably pretty near the truth. That sort of thing's worth diamonds to a writer.'

She laughed. 'You mean that . . . diamonds?'

Bond said: 'Well, I don't earn all that as a writer, but I've already sold an option on this story for a film, and if I can make it authentic enough I dare say they'll actually buy the film.' He reached out and put his hand over hers in her lap. She did not take her hand away. 'Yes, diamonds. A diamond clip from Van Cleef. Is it a deal?'

Now she took her hand away. They were arriving at the Ambassadori. She picked up her bag from the seat beside her. She turned on the seat so that she faced him. The commissionaire opened the door and the light from the street turned her eyes into stars. She examined his face with a certain seriousness. She said: 'All men are pigs, but some are lesser pigs than others. All right. I will meet you. But not for dinner. What I may tell you is not for public places. I bathe every afternoon at the Lido. But not at the fashionable plage. I bathe at the Bagni Alberoni, where the English poet Byron used to ride his horse. It is at the tip of the peninsula. The Vaporetto will take you there. You will find me there the day after tomorrow—at three in the afternoon. I shall be getting my last sunburn before the winter. Among the sand-dunes. You will see a pale yellow umbrella. Underneath it will be me.' She smiled. 'Knock on the umbrella and ask for Fräulein Lisl Baum.'

She got out of the taxi. Bond followed. She held out her hand. 'Thank you for coming to my rescue. Goodnight.'

Bond said: 'Three o'clock then. I shall be there. Goodnight.'

She turned and walked up the curved steps of the hotel. Bond looked after her thoughtfully, and then turned and got back into the taxi and told the man to take him to the Nazionale. He sat back and watched the neon signs ribbon past the window. Things, including the taxi, were going almost too fast for comfort. The only one over which he had any control was the taxi. He leant forward and told the man to drive more slowly.

The best train from Rome to Venice is the Laguna express that leaves every day at midday. Bond, after a morning that was chiefly occupied with difficult talks with his London Headquarters on Station I's scrambler, caught it by the skin of his teeth. The Laguna is a smart, streamlined affair that looks and sounds more luxurious than it is. The seats are made for small Italians and the restaurant car staff suffer from the disease that afflicts their brethren in the great trains all over the world—a genuine loathing for the modern traveller and particularly for the foreigner. Bond had a gangway seat over the axle in the rear aluminium coach. If the seven heavens had been flowing by outside the window he would not have cared. He kept his eyes inside the train, read a jerking book, spilled Chianti over the tablecloth and shifted his long, aching legs and cursed the Ferrovie Italiane dello Stato.

But at last there was Mestre and the dead straight finger of rail across the eighteenth century aquatint into Venice. Then came the unfailing shock of the beauty that never betrays and the soft swaying progress down the Grand Canal into a blood-red sunset, and the extreme pleasure—so it seemed—of the Gritti Palace that Bond should have ordered the best double room on the first floor.

That evening, scattering thousand-lira notes like leaves in Vallombrosa, James Bond sought, at Harry's Bar, at Florian's, and finally upstairs in the admirable Quadri, to establish to anyone who might be interested that he was what he had wished to appear to the girl—a prosperous writer who lived high and well. Then, in the temporary state of euphoria that a first night in Venice engenders, however high and serious the purpose of the visitor, James Bond walked back to the Gritti and had eight hours dreamless sleep.

May and October are the best months in Venice. The sun is soft and the nights are cool. The glittering scene is kinder to the eyes and there is a freshness in the air that helps one to hammer out those long miles of stone and terrazza and marble that are intolerable to the feet in summer. And there are fewer people. Although Venice is the one town in the world that can swallow up a hundred thousand tourists as easily as it can a thousand—hiding them down its side-streets, using them for crowd scenes on the piazzas, stuffing them into the vaporetti—it is still better to share Venice with the minimum number of packaged tours and Lederhosen.

Bond spent the next morning strolling the backstreets in the hope that he would be able to uncover a tail. He visited a couple of churches—not to admire their interiors but to discover if anyone came in after him through the main entrance before he left by the side door. No one was following him. Bond went to Florian's and had an Americano and listened to a couple of French culture-snobs discussing the imbalance of the containing façade of St Mark's Square. On an impulse, he bought a postcard and sent it off to his secretary who had once been with the Georgian Group to Italy and had never allowed Bond to forget it. He wrote: "Venice is wonderful. Have so far inspected the railway station and the Stock Exchange. Very aesthetically satisfying. To the Municipal Waterworks this afternoon and then an old Brigitte Bardot at the Scala Cinema. Do you know a wonderful tune called 'O Sole Mio?' It's v. romantic like everything here. JB.'

Pleased with his inspiration, Bond had an early luncheon and went back to his hotel. He locked the door of his room and took off his coat and ran over the Walther PPK. He put up the safe and practised one or two quick draws and put the gun back in the holster. It was time to go. He went along to the landing-stage and boarded the twelve-forty vaporetto to Alberoni, out of sight across the mirrored lagoons. Then he set-

tled down in a seat in the bows and wondered what was going
to happen to him.

From the jetty at Alberoni, on the Venice side of the Lido
peninsula, there is a half mile dusty walk across the neck of
land to the Bagni Alberoni facing the Adriatic. It is a curiously
deserted world, this tip of the famous peninsula. A mile down
the thin neck of land the luxury real estate development has
petered out in a scattering of cracked stucco villas and bank-
rupt housing projects, and here there is nothing but the tiny
fishing village of Alberoni, a sanatorium for students, a
derelict experimental station belonging to the Italian Navy
and some massive weed-choked gun emplacements from the
last war. In the no man's land in the centre of this thin tongue
of land is the Golf du Lido, whose brownish undulating fair-
ways meander around the ruins of ancient fortifications. Not
many people come to Venice to play golf, and the project is
kept alive for its snob appeal by the grand hotels of the Lido.
The golf course is surrounded by a high wire fence hung at intervals, as if it protected something of great value or secrecy,
with threatening Vietatos and Prohibitos. Around this wired
enclave, the scrub and sandhills have not even been cleared
of mines, and amongst the rusting barbed wire are signs saying MINAS. PERICOLO DI MORTE beneath a roughly stencilled skull
and crossbones. The whole area is strange and melancholy
and in extraordinary contrast to the gay carnival world of
Venice less than an hour away across the lagoons.

Bond was sweating slightly by the time he had walked the
half mile across the peninsula to the plage, and he stood for a
moment under the last of the acacia trees that had bordered
the dusty road to cool off while he got his bearings. In front of
him was a rickety wooden archway whose central span said
BAGNI ALBERONI in faded blue paint. Beyond were the lines of
equally dilapidated wooden cabins, and then a hundred yards

of sand and then the quiet blue glass of the sea. There were
no bathers and the place seemed to be closed, but when he
walked through the archway he heard the tinny sound of a
radio playing Neapolitan music. It came from a ramshackle
hut that advertised Coca-Cola and various Italian soft drinks.
Deck-chairs were stacked against its walls and there were
two pedallos and a child's half inflated seahorse. The whole
establishment looked so derelict that Bond could not imagine it doing business even at the height of the summer season. He stepped off the narrow duckboards into the soft,
burned sand and moved round behind the huts to the beach.
He walked down to the edge of the sea. To the left, until it
disappeared in the autumn heat haze, the wide empty sand
swept away in a slight curve towards the Lido proper. To the
right was half a mile of beach terminating in the seawall at
the tip of the peninsula. The seawall stretched like a finger
out into the silent mirrored sea, and at intervals along its top
were the flimsy derricks of the octopus fishermen. Behind
the beach were the sandhills and a section of the wire fence
surrounding the golf course. On the edge of the sandhills,
perhaps five hundred yards away, there was a speck of bright
yellow.

Bond set off towards it along the tide-line.

'Ahem.'

The hands flew to the top scrap of bikini and pulled it up.
Bond walked into her line of vision and stood looking down.
The bright shadow of the umbrella covered only her face. The
rest of her—a burned cream body in a black bikini on a black
and white striped bath-towel—lay offered to the sun.

She looked up at him through half closed eyelashes. 'You
are five minutes early and I told you to knock.'

Bond sat down close to her in the shade of the big umbrella.
He took out a handkerchief and wiped his face. 'You happen
to own the only palm tree in the whole of this desert. I had to

get underneath it as soon as I could. This is the hell of a place for a rendezvous.'

She laughed. 'I am like Greta Garbo. I like to be alone.'

'Are we alone?'

She opened her eyes wide. 'Why not? You think I have brought a chaperone?'

'Since you think all men are pigs . . .'

'Ah, but you are a gentleman pig,' she giggled. 'A milord pig. And anyway, it is too hot for that kind of thing. And there is too much sand. And besides this is a business meeting, no? I tell you stories about drugs and you give me a diamond clip. From Van Cleef. Or have you changed your mind?'

'No. That's how it is. Where shall we begin?'

'You ask the questions. What is it you want to know?' She sat up and pulled her knees to her between her arms. Flirtation had gone out of her eyes and they had become attentive, and perhaps a little careful.

Bond noticed the change. He said casually, watching her: 'They say your friend Colombo is a big man in the game. Tell me about him. He would make a good character for my book—disguised, of course. But it's the detail I need. How does he operate, and so on? That's not the sort of thing a writer can invent.'

She veiled her eyes. She said: 'Enrico would be very angry if he knew that I had told any of his secrets. I don't know what he would do to me.'

'He will never know.'

She looked at him seriously. 'Lieber Mr Bond, there is very little that he does not know. And he is also quite capable of acting on a guess. I would not be surprised'—Bond caught her quick glance at his watch— if it had crossed his mind to have me followed here. He is a very suspicious man.' She put her hand out and touched his sleeve. Now she looked nervous. She said urgently: 'I think you had better go now. This has been a great mistake.'

Bond openly looked at his watch. It was three-thirty. He moved his head so that he could look behind the umbrella and back down the beach. Far down by the bathing huts, their outlines dancing slightly in the heat haze, were three men in dark clothes. They were walking purposefully up the beach, their feet keeping step as if they were a squad.

Bond got to his feet. He looked down at the bent head. He said drily: 'I see what you mean. Just tell Colombo that from now on I'm writing his life-story. And I'm a very persistent writer. So long.' Bond started running up the sand towards the tip of the peninsula. From there he could double back down the other shore to the village and the safety of people.

Down the beach the three men broke into a fast jog-trot, elbows and legs pounding in time with each other as if they were long-distance runners out for a training spin. As they jogged past the girl, one of the men raised a hand. She raised hers in answer and then lay down on the sand and turned over—perhaps so that her back could now get its toasting, or perhaps because she did not want to watch the man-hunt.

Bond took off his tie as he ran and put it in his pocket. It was very hot and he was already sweating profusely. But so would the three men be. It was a question who was in better training. At the tip of the peninsula, Bond clambered up on to the seawall and looked back. The men had hardly gained, but now two of them were fanning out to cut round the edge of the golf course boundary. They did not seem to mind the danger notices with the skull and crossbones. Bond, running fast down the wide seawall, measured angles and distances. The two men were cutting across the base of the triangle. It was going to be a close call.

Bond's shirt was already soaked and his feet were beginning to hurt. He had run perhaps a mile. How much farther to safety? At intervals along the seawall the breeches of antique cannon had been sunk in the concrete. They would be

mooring posts for the fishing fleets sheltering in the protection of the lagoons before taking to the Adriatic. Bond
counted his steps between two of them. Fifty yards. How
many black knobs to the end of the wall—to the first houses
of the village? Bond counted up to thirty before the line vanished into the heat haze. Probably another mile to go. Could
he do it, and fast enough to beat the two flankers? Bond's
breath was already rasping in his throat. Now even his suit
was soaked with sweat and the cloth of his trousers was chaf-
ing his legs. Behind him, three hundred yards back, was one
pursuer. To his right, dodging among the sand-dunes and
converging fast, were the other two. To his left was a twenty-
foot slope of masonry to the green tide ripping out into the
Adriatic.

Bond was planning to slow down to a walk and keep
enough breath to try and shoot it out with the three men,
when two things happened in quick succession. First he saw
through the haze ahead a group of spear-fishermen. There
were about half a dozen of them, some in the water and some
sunning themselves on the seawall. Then from the sand-
dunes came the deep roar of an explosion. Earth and scrub
and what might have been bits of a man fountained briefly
into the air, and a small shock-wave hit him. Bond slowed.
The other man in the dunes had stopped. He was standing
stock-still. His mouth was open and a frightened jabber came
from it. Suddenly he collapsed on the ground with his arms
wapped round his head. Bond knew the signs. He would not
move again until someone came and carried him away from
there. Bond's heart lifted. Now he had only about two hundred yards to go to the fishermen. They were already gathering into a group, looking towards him. Bond summoned a few
words of Italian and rehearsed them. 'Mi Ingles. Prego, dove il
carabinieri.' Bond glanced over his shoulder. Odd, but despite
the witnessing spear-fishers, the man was still coming on. He

had gained and was only about a hundred yards behind. There was a gun in his hand. Now, ahead, the fishermen had fanned out across Bond's path. They had harpoon guns held at the ready. In the centre was a big man with a tiny red bathing-slip hanging beneath his stomach. A green mask was slipped back on to the crown of his head. He stood with his blue swim-fins pointing out and his arms akimbo. He looked like Mr Toad of Toad Hall in Technicolor. Bond's amused thought died in him stillborn. Panting, he slowed to a walk. Automatically his sweaty hand felt under his coat for the gun and drew it out. The man in the centre of the arc of pointing harpoons was Enrico Colombo.

Colombo watched him approach. When he was twenty yards away, Colombo said quietly: 'Put away your toy, Mr Bond of the Secret Service. These are CO_2 harpoon guns. And stay where you are. Unless you wish to make a copy of Mantegna's St Sebastian.' He turned to the man on his right. He spoke in English. 'At what range was that Albanian last week?'

'Twenty yards, padrone. And the harpoon went right through. But he was a fat man—perhaps twice as thick as this one.'

Bond stopped. One of the iron bollards was beside him. He sat down and rested the gun on his knee. It pointed at the centre of Colombo's big stomach. He said: 'Five harpoons in me won't stop one bullet in you, Colombo.'

Colombo smiled and nodded, and the man who had been coming softly up behind Bond hit him once hard in the base of the skull with the butt of his Luger.

When you come to from being hit on the head the first reaction is a fit of vomiting. Even in his wretchedness Bond was aware of two sensations—he was in a ship at sea, and someone, a man, was wiping his forehead with a cool wet towel and murmuring encouragement in bad English. 'Is okay, amigo. Take him easy. Take him easy.'

Bond fell back on his bunk, exhausted. It was a comfortable small cabin with a feminine smell and dainty curtains and colours. A sailor in a tattered vest and trousers—Bond thought he recognized him as one of the spear-fishermen—was bending over him. He smiled when Bond opened his eyes. 'Is better, yes? Subito okay.' He rubbed the back of his neck in sympathy. 'It hurts for a little. Soon it will only be a black. Beneath the hair. The girls will see nothing.'

Bond smiled feebly and nodded. The pain of the nod made him screw up his eyes. When he opened them the sailor shook his head in admonition. He brought his wrist-watch close up to Bond's eyes. It said seven o'clock. He pointed with his little finger at the figure nine. 'Mangiare con Padrone, Si?'

Bond said: 'Si.'

The man put his hand to his cheek and laid his head on one side. 'Dormire.'

Bond said 'Si' again and the sailor went out of the cabin and closed the door without locking it.

Bond got gingerly off the bunk and went over to the wash basin and set about cleaning himself. On top of the chest of drawers was a neat pile of his personal belongings. Everything was there except his gun. Bond stowed the things away in his pockets, and sat down again on the bunk and smoked and thought. His thoughts were totally inconclusive. He was being taken for a ride, or rather a sail, but from the behaviour of the sailor it did not seem that he was regarded as an enemy. Yet a great deal of trouble had been taken to make him prisoner and one of Colombo's men had even, though inadvertently, died in the process. It did not seem to be just a question of killing him. Perhaps this soft treatment was the preliminary to trying to make a deal with him. What was the deal—and what was the alternative?

At nine o'clock the same sailor came for Bond and led him down a short passage to a small, blowzy saloon, and left him. There was a table and two chairs in the middle of the room, and beside the table a nickel-plated trolley laden with food and drinks. Bond tried the hatchway at the end of the saloon. It was bolted. He unlatched one of the portholes and looked out. There was just enough light to see that the ship was about two hundred tons and might once have been a large fishing-vessel. The engine sounded like a single diesel and they were carrying sail. Bond estimated the ship's speed at six or seven knots. On the dark horizon there was a tiny cluster of yellow lights. It seemed probable that they were sailing down the Adriatic coast.

The hatchway bolt rattled back. Bond pulled in his head. Colombo came down the steps. He was dressed in a sweat-shirt, dungarees and scuffed sandals. There was a wicked, amused gleam in his eyes. He sat down in one chair and waved to the other. 'Come, my friend. Food and drink and plenty of talk. We will now stop behaving like little boys and be grown-up. Yes? What will you have—gin, whisky, champagne? And this is the finest sausage in the whole of Bologna. Olives from my own estate. Bread, butter, Provelone—that is smoked cheese—and fresh figs. Peasant food, but good. Come. All that running must have given you an appetite.'

His laugh was infectious. Bond poured himself a stiff whisky and soda, and sat down. He said: 'Why did you have to go to so much trouble? We could have met without all these dramatics. As it is you have prepared a lot of grief for yourself. I warned my chief that something like this might happen—the way the girl picked me up in your restaurant was too childish for words. I said that I would walk into the trap to see what it was all about. If I am not out of it again by tomorrow midday, you'll have Interpol as well as Italian police on top of you like a load of bricks.'

Colombo looked puzzled. He said: 'If you were ready to walk into the trap, why did you try and escape from my men this afternoon? I had sent them to fetch you and bring you to my ship, and it would all have been much more friendly. Now I have lost a good man and you might easily have had your skull broken. I do not understand.'

'I didn't like the look of those three men. I know killers when I see them. I thought you might be thinking of doing something stupid. You should have used the girl. The men were unnecessary.'

Colombo shook his head. 'Lisl was willing to find out more about you, but nothing else. She will now be just as angry with me as you are. Life is very difficult. I like to be friends with everyone, and now I have made two enemies in one afternoon. It is too bad.' Colombo looked genuinely sorry for himself. He cut a thick slice of sausage, impatiently tore the rind off it with his teeth and began to eat. While his mouth was still full he took a glass of champagne and washed the sausage down with it. He said, shaking his head reproachfully at Bond: 'It is always the same, when I am worried I have to eat. But the food that I eat when I am worried I cannot digest. And now you have worried me. You say that we could have met and talked things over—that I need not have taken all this trouble.' He spread his hands helplessly. 'How was I to know that? By saying that, you put the blood of Mario on my hands. I did not tell him to take a short cut through that place.' Colombo pounded the table. Now he shouted angrily at Bond. 'I do not agree that this was all my fault. It was your fault. Yours only. You had agreed to kill me. How does one arrange a friendly meeting with one's murderer? Eh? Just tell me that.' Colombo snatched up a long roll of bread and stuffed it into his mouth, his eyes furious.

'What the hell are you talking about?'

Colombo threw the remains of the roll on the table and got

to his feet, holding Bond's eyes locked in his. He walked sideways, still gazing fixedly at Bond, to a chest of drawers, felt for the knob of the top drawer, opened it, groped and lifted out what Bond recognized as a tape-recorder playback machine. Still looking accusingly at Bond, he brought the machine over to the table. He sat down and pressed a switch.

When Bond heard the voice he picked up his glass of whisky and looked into it. The tinny voice said: 'Exact. Now, before I give you the informations, like good commercials we make the terms. Yes?' The voice went on: 'Ten thousand dollars American . . . There is no telling where you get these informations from. Even if you are beaten . . . The head of this machina is a bad man. He is to be destrutto—killed.' Bond waited for his own voice to break through the restaurant noises. There had been a long pause while he thought about the last condition. What was it he had said? His voice came out of the machine, answering him. 'I cannot promise that. You must see that. All I can say is that if the man tries to destroy me, I will destroy him.'

Colombo switched off the machine. Bond swallowed down his whisky. Now he could look up at Colombo. He said defensively: 'That doesn't make me a murderer.'

Colombo looked at him sorrowfully. 'To me it does. Coming from an Englishman. I worked for the English during the War. In the Resistance. I have the King's Medal.' He put his hand in his pocket and threw the silver Freedom medal with the red, white and blue striped ribbon on to the table. 'You see?'

Bond obstinately held Colombo's eyes. He said: 'And the rest of the stuff on that tape? You long ago stopped working for the English. Now you work against them, for money.'

Colombo grunted. He tapped the machine with his forefinger. He said impassively: 'I have heard it all. It is lies.' He banged his fist on the table so that the glasses jumped. He bellowed furiously: 'It is lies, lies. Every word of it.' He jumped

to his feet. His chair crashed down behind him. He slowly
bent and picked it up. He reached for the whisky bottle and
walked round and poured four fingers into Bond's glass. He
went back to his chair and sat down and put the champagne
bottle on the table in front of him. Now his face was com-
posed, serious. He said quietly: 'It is not all lies. There is a
grain of truth in what that bastard told you. That is why I decided not to argue with you. You might not have believed me.
You would have dragged in the police. There would have
been much trouble for me and my comrades. Even if you or
someone else had not found reason to kill me, there would
have been scandal, ruin. Instead I decided to show you the
truth—the truth you were sent to Italy to find out. Within a
matter of hours, tomorrow at dawn, your mission will have
been completed.' Colombo clicked his fingers. 'Presto—like
that.'

Bond said: 'What part of Kristatos's story is not lies?'

Colombo's eyes looked into Bond's calculating. Finally he
said: 'My friend, I am a smuggler. That part is true. I am probably the most successful smuggler in the Mediterranean. Half
the American cigarettes in Italy are brought in by me from
Tangier. Gold? I am the sole supplier of the black valuta market. Diamonds? I have my own purveyor in Beirut with direct
lines to Sierra Leone and South Africa. In the old days, when
these things were scarce, I also handled aureomycin and peni-
cillin and such medicines. Bribery at the American base hos-
pitals. And there have been many other things—even
beautiful girls from Syria and Persia for the houses of Naples.
I have also smuggled out escaped convicts. But,' Colombo's
fist crashed on the table, 'drugs, heroin, opium, hemp—no!
Never! I will have nothing to do with these things. These
things are evil. There is no sin in the others.' Colombo held up
his right hand. 'My friend, this I swear to you on the head of
my mother.'

Bond was beginning to see daylight. He was prepared to believe Colombo. He even felt a curious liking for this greedy,
boisterous pirate who had so nearly been put on the spot by
Kristatos. Bond said: 'But why did Kristatos put the finger on
you? What's he got to gain?'

Colombo slowly shook a finger to and fro in front of his
nose. He said: 'My friend, Kristatos is Kristatos. He is playing
the biggest double game it is possible to conceive. To keep it
up—to keep the protection of American Intelligence and their
Narcotics people—he must now and then throw them a victim—
some small man on the fringe of the big game. But with this
English problem it is different. That is a huge traffic. To protect it, a big victim was required. I was chosen—by Kristatos,
or by his employers. And it is true that if you had been vigor-
ous in your investigations and had spent enough hard currency on buying information, you might have discovered the
story of my operations. But each trail towards *me* would have
led you further away from the truth. In the end, for I do not
underestimate your Service, I would have gone to prison. But
the big fox you are after would only be laughing at the sound
of the hunt dying away in the distance.'

'Why did Kristatos want you killed?'

Colombo looked cunning. 'My friend, I know too much. In
the fraternity of smugglers, we occasionally stumble on a corner of the next man's business. Not long ago, in this ship, I had
a running fight with a small gunboat from Albania. A lucky
shot set fire to their fuel. There was only one survivor. He was
persuaded to talk. I learnt much, but like a fool I took a chance
with the minefields and set him ashore on the coast north of
Tirana. It was a mistake. Ever since then I have had this bastard Kristatos after me. Fortunately,' Colombo grinned
wolfishly, 'I have one piece of information he does not know
of. And we have a rendezvous with this piece of information
at first light tomorrow—at a small fishing-port just north of

Ancona, Santa Maria. And there,' Colombo gave a harsh, cruel laugh, 'we shall see what we shall see.'

Bond said mildly, 'What's your price for all this? You say my mission will have been completed tomorrow morning. How much?'

Colombo shook his head. He said indifferently: 'Nothing. It just happens that our interests coincide. But I shall need your promise that what I have told you this evening is between you and me and, if necessary, your Chief in London. It must never come back to Italy. Is that agreed?'

'Yes. I agree to that.'

Colombo got to his feet. He went to the chest of drawers and took out Bond's gun. He handed it to Bond 'In that case, my friend, you had better have this, because you are going to need it. And you had better get some sleep. There will be rum and coffee for everyone at five in the morning.' He held out his hand. Bond took it. Suddenly the two men were friends. Bond felt the fact. He said awkwardly 'All right, Colombo,' and went out of the saloon and along to his cabin.

The *Colombina* had a crew of twelve. They were youngish, tough-looking men. They talked softly among themselves as the mugs of hot coffee and rum were dished out by Colombo in the saloon. A storm lantern was the only light—the ship had been darkened—and Bond smiled to himself at the Treasure Island atmosphere of excitement and conspiracy. Colombo went from man to man on a weapon inspection. They all had Lugers, carried under the jersey inside the trouser-band, and flick-knives in the pocket. Colombo had a word of approval or criticism for each weapon. It struck Bond that Colombo had made a good life for himself—a life of adventure and thrill and risk. It was a criminal life—a running fight with the currency laws, the State tobacco monopoly, the Customs, the police—but there was a whiff of adolescent rascality in the air which somehow changed the colour of the crime from black to white—or at least to grey.

Colombo looked at his watch. He dismissed the men to their posts. He dowsed the lantern and, in the oyster light of dawn, Bond followed him up to the bridge. He found the ship was close to a black, rocky shore which they were following at reduced speed. Colombo pointed ahead. 'Round that headland is the harbour. Our approach will not have been observed. In the harbour, against the jetty, I expect to find a ship of about this size unloading innocent rolls of newsprint down a ramp into a warehouse. Round the headland, we will put on full speed and come alongside this ship and board her. There will be resistance. Heads will be broken. I hope it is not shooting. We shall not shoot unless they do. But it will be an Albanian ship manned by a crew of Albanian toughs. If there is shooting, you must shoot well with the rest of us. These people are enemies of your country as well as mine. If you get killed, you get killed. Okay?'

'That's all right.'

As Bond said the words, there came a ting on the engine-room telegraph and the deck began to tremble under his feet. Making ten knots, the small ship rounded the headland into the harbour.

It was as Colombo had said. Alongside a stone jetty lay the ship, its sails flapping idly. From her stern a ramp of wood planks sloped down towards the dark mouth of a ramshackle corrugated iron warehouse, inside which burned feeble electric lights. The ship carried a deck cargo of what appeared to be rolls of newsprint, and these were being hoisted one by one on to the ramp whence they rolled down under their own momentum through the mouth of the warehouse. There were about twenty men in sight. Only surprise would straighten out these odds. Now Colombo's craft was fifty yards away from the other ship, and one or two of the men had stopped work-

ing and were looking in their direction. One man ran off into
the warehouse. Simultaneously Colombo issued a sharp order.
The engines stopped and went into reverse. A big searchlight
on the bridge came on and lit the whole scene brightly as the
ship drifted up alongside the Albanian trawler. At the first
hard contact, grappling-irons were tossed over the Albanian's
rail fore and aft, and Colombo's men swarmed over the side
with Colombo in the lead.

Bond had made his own plans. As soon as his feet landed
on the enemy deck, he ran straight across the ship, climbed
the far rail and jumped. It was about twelve feet to the jetty
and he landed like a cat, on his hands and toes, and stayed for
a moment, crouching, planning his next move. Shooting had
already started on deck. An early shot killed the searchlight
and now there was only the grey, luminous light of dawn. A
body, one of the enemy, crunched to the stone in front of him
and lay spread-eagled, motionless. At the same time, from the
mouth of the warehouse, a light machine gun started up, firing short bursts with a highly professional touch. Bond ran towards it in the dark shadow of the ship. The machine-gunner
saw him and gave him a burst. The bullets zipped round
Bond, clanged against the iron hull of the ship and whined off
into the night. Bond got to the cover of the sloping ramp of
boards and dived forward on his stomach. The bullets crashed
into the wood above his head. Bond crept forward into the
narrowing space. When he had got as close as he could, he
would have a choice of breaking cover either to right or left of
the boards. There came a series of heavy thuds and a swift
rumble above his head. One of Colombo's men must have cut
the ropes and sent the whole pile of newsprint rolls down the
ramp. Now was Bond's chance. He leapt out from under
cover—to the left. If the machine-gunner was waiting for him,
he would expect Bond to come out firing on the right. The
machine-gunner was there, crouching up against the wall of

the warehouse. Bond fired twice in the split second before the bright muzzle of the enemy weapon had swung through its small arc. The dead man's finger clenched on the trigger and, as he slumped, his gun made a brief Catherine-wheel of flashes before it shook itself free from his hand and clattered to the ground.

Bond was running forward towards the warehouse door when he slipped and fell headlong. He lay for a moment, stunned, his face in a pool of black treacle. He cursed and got to his hands and knees and made a dash for cover behind a jumble of the big newsprint rolls that had crashed into the wall of the warehouse. One of them, sliced by a burst from the machine gun, was leaking black treacle. Bond wiped as much of the stuff off his hands and face as he could. It had the musty sweet smell that Bond had once smelled in Mexico. It was raw opium.

A bullet whanged into the wall of the warehouse not far from his head. Bond gave his gun-hand a last wipe on the seat of his trousers and leapt for the warehouse door. He was surprised not to be shot at from the interior as soon as he was silhouetted against the entrance. It was quiet and cool inside the place. The lights had been turned out, but it was now getting brighter outside. The pale newsprint rolls were stacked in orderly ranks with a space to make a passageway down the centre. At the far end of the passageway was a door. The whole arrangement leered at him, daring him. Bond smelled death. He edged back to the entrance and out into the open. The shooting had become spasmodic. Colombo came running swiftly towards him, his feet close to the ground as fat men run. Bond said peremptorily: 'Stay at this door. Don't go in or let any of your men in. I'm going round to the back.' Without waiting for an answer he sprinted round the corner of the building and down along its side.

The warehouse was about fifty feet long. Bond slowed and

walked softly to the far corner. He flattened himself against the corrugated iron wall and took a swift look round. He immediately drew back. A man was standing up against the back entrance. His eyes were at some kind of spyhole. In his hand was a plunger from which wires ran under the bottom of the door. A car, a black Lancia Granturismo convertible with the hood down, stood beside him, its engine ticking over softly. It pointed inland along a deeply tracked dust road.

The man was Kristatos.

Bond knelt. He held his gun in both hands for steadiness, inched swiftly round the corner of the building and fired one shot at the man's feet. He missed. Almost as he saw the dust kick up inches off the target, there was the rumbling crack of an explosion and the tin wall hit him and sent him flying.

Bond scrambled to his feet. The warehouse had buckled crazily out of shape. Now it started to collapse noisily like a pack of tin cards. Kristatos was in the car. It was already twenty yards away, dust fountaining up from the traction on the rear wheels. Bond stood in the classic pistol-shooting pose and took careful aim. The Walther roared and kicked three times. At the last shot, at fifty yards, the figure crouched over the wheel jerked backwards. The hands flew sideways off the wheel. The head craned briefly into the air and slumped forward. The right hand remained sticking out as if the dead man was signalling a right-hand turn. Bond started to run up the road expecting the car to stop, but the wheels were held in the ruts and, with the weight of the dead right foot still on the accelerator, the Lancia tore onwards in its screaming third gear. Bond stopped and watched it. It hurried on along the flat road across the burned-up plain and the cloud of white dust blew gaily up behind. At any moment Bond expected it to veer off the road, but it did not, and Bond stood and saw it out of sight into the early morning mist that promised a beautiful day.

Bond put his gun on safe and tucked it away in the belt of his trousers. He turned to find Colombo approaching him. The fat man was grinning delightedly. He came up with Bond and, to Bond's horror, threw open his arms, clutched Bond to him and kissed him on both cheeks.

Bond said: 'For God's sake, Colombo.'

Colombo roared with laughter. 'Ah, the quiet Englishman! He fears nothing save the emotions. But me,' he hit himself in the chest, 'me, Enrico Colombo, loves this man and he is not ashamed to say so. If you had not got the machine-gunner, not one of us would have survived. As it is, I lost two of my men and others have wounds. But only half a dozen Albanians remain on their feet and they have escaped into the village. No doubt the police will round them up. And now you have sent that bastard Kristatos motoring down to hell. What a splendid finish to him! What will happen when the little racing-hearse meets the main road? He is already signalling for the right-hand turn on to the autostrada, I hope he will remember to drive on the right.' Colombo clapped Bond boisterously on the shoulder. 'But come, my friend. It is time we got out of here. The cocks are open in the Albanian ship and she will soon be on the bottom. There are no telephones in this little place. We will have a good start on the police. It will take them some time to get sense out of the fishermen. I have spoken to the head man. No one here has any love for Albanians. But we must be on our way. We have a stiff sail into the wind and there is no doctor I can trust this side of Venice.'

Flames were beginning to lick out of the shattered warehouse, and there was billowing smoke that smelled of sweet vegetables. Bond and Colombo walked round to windward. The Albanian ship had settled on the bottom and her decks were awash. They waded across her and climbed on board the *Colombina*, where Bond had to go through some more handshaking and backslapping. They cast off at once and made for

the headland guarding the harbour. There was a small group
of fishermen standing by their boats that lay drawn up on the
beach below a huddle of stone cottages. They made a surly
impression, but when Colombo waved and shouted something in Italian most of them raised a hand in farewell, and
one of them called back something that made the crew of the
Colombina laugh. Colombo explained: 'They say we were better than the cinema at Ancona and we must come again soon.'

Bond suddenly felt the excitement drain out of him. He felt
dirty and unshaven, and he could smell his own sweat. He
went below and borrowed a razor and a clean shirt from one
of the crew, and stripped in his cabin and cleansed himself.
When he took out his gun and threw it on the bunk he caught
a whiff of cordite from the barrel. It brought back the fear and
violence and death of the grey dawn. He opened the porthole.
Outside, the sea was dancing and gay, and the receding coast-
line, that had been black and mysterious, was now green and
beautiful. A sudden delicious scent of frying bacon came
downwind from the galley. Abruptly Bond pulled the porthole to and dressed and went along to the saloon.

Over a mound of fried eggs and bacon washed down with
hot sweet coffee laced with rum, Colombo dotted the i's and
crossed the t's.

'This we have done, my friend,' he said through crunching
toast. 'That was a year's supply of raw opium on its way to
Kristatos's chemical works in Naples. It is true that I have
such a business in Milan and that it is a convenient depot for
some of my wares. But it fabricates nothing more deadly than
cascara and aspirin. For all that part of Kristatos's story, read
Kristatos instead of Colombo. It is he who breaks the stuff
down into heroin and it is he who employs the couriers to
take it to London. That huge shipment was worth perhaps a
million pounds to Kristatos and his men. But do you know
something, my dear James? It cost him not one solitary cent.

Why? Because it is a gift from Russia. The gift of a massive
and deadly projectile to be fired into the bowels of England.
The Russians can supply unlimited quantities of the charge
for the projectile. It comes from their poppy fields in the Cau-
casus, and Albania is a convenient entrepôt. But they have not
the apparatus to fire this projectile. The man Kristatos created
the necessary apparatus, and it is he, on behalf of his masters
in Russia, who pulls the trigger. Today, between us, we have
destroyed, in half an hour, the entire conspiracy. You can now
go back and tell your people in England that the traffic will
cease. You can also tell them the truth—that Italy was not the
origin of this terrible underground weapon of war. That it is
our old friends the Russians. No doubt it is some psychological warfare section of their Intelligence apparatus. That I cannot tell you. Perhaps, my dear James,' Colombo smiled
encouragingly, 'they will send you to Moscow to find out. If
that should happen, let us hope you will find some girl as
charming as your friend Fräulein Lisl Baum to put you on the
right road to the truth.'

'What do you mean "my friend"? She's yours.'

Colombo shook his head. 'My dear James, I have many
friends. You will be spending a few more days in Italy writing
your report, and no doubt,' he chuckled, 'checking on some of
the things I have told you. Perhaps you will also have an en-
joyable half an hour explaining the facts of life to your col-
leagues in American Intelligence. In between these duties you
will need companionship—someone to show you the beauties
of my beloved homeland. In uncivilized countries, it is the polite custom to offer one of your wives to a man whom you love
and wish to honour. I also am uncivilized. I have no wives,
but I have many such friends as Lisl Baum. She will not need
to receive any instructions in this matter. I have good reason
to believe that she is awaiting your return this evening.'
Colombo fished in his trousers pocket and tossed something

down with a clang on the table in front of Bond. 'Here is the good reason.' Colombo put his hand to his heart and looked seriously into Bond's eyes. 'I give it to you from my heart. Perhaps also from hers.'

Bond picked the thing up. It was a key with a heavy metal tag attached. The metal tag was inscribed *Albergo Danielli. Room 68*.

The sting-ray was about six feet from wing-tip to wing-tip, and perhaps ten feet long from the blunt wedge of its nose to the end of its deadly tail. It was dark grey with that violet tinge that is so often a danger signal in the underwater world. When it rose up from the pale golden sand and swam a little distance it was as if a black towel was being waved through the water.

James Bond, his hands along his flanks and swimming with only a soft trudge of his fins, followed the black shadow across the wide palm-fringed lagoon, waiting for a shot. He rarely killed fish except to eat, but there were exceptions—big moray eels and all the members of the scorpion-fish family. Now he proposed to kill the sting-ray because it looked so extraordinarily evil.

It was ten o'clock in the morning of a day in April, and the lagoon, Belle Anse near the southernmost tip of Mahe, the largest island in the Seychelles group, was glassy calm. The north-west monsoon had blown itself out months before and it would be May before the south-east monsoon brought refreshment. Now the temperature was eighty in the shade and the humidity ninety, and in the enclosed waters of the lagoon the water was near blood heat. Even the fish seemed to be sluggish. A ten-pound green parrot-fish, nibbling algae from a lump of coral, paused only to roll its eyes as Bond passed overhead, and then went back to its meal. A school of fat grey chub, swimming busily, broke courteously in half to let Bond's shadow by, and then joined up and continued on their opposite course. A chorus line of six small squids, normally as shy as birds, did not even bother to change their camouflage at his passage.

Bond trudged lazily on, keeping the sting-ray just in sight. Soon it would get tired or else be reassured when Bond, the big fish on the surface, did not attack. Then it would settle on to a patch of flat sand, change its camouflage down to the palest, almost translucent grey, and, with soft undulations of its wing-tips, bury itself in the sand.

The reef was coming nearer and now there were outcrops of coral niggerheads and meadows of sea-grass. It was like arriving in a town from open country. Everywhere the jewelled reef fish twinkled and glowed and the giant anemones of the Indian Ocean burned like flames in the shadows. Colonies of spined sea-eggs made sepia splashes as if someone had thrown ink against the rock, and the brilliant blue and yellow feelers of langoustes quested and waved from their crevices like small dragons. Now and then, among the seaweed on the brilliant floor, there was the speckled glitter of a cowrie bigger than a golf ball—the leopard cowrie—and once Bond saw the beautiful splayed fingers of a Venus's harp. But all these things were now commonplace to him and he drove steadily on, interested in the reef only as cover through which he could get to seaward of the ray and then pursue it back towards the shore. The tactic worked, and soon the black shadow with its pursuing brown torpedo were moving back across the great blue mirror. In about twelve feet of water the ray stopped for the hundredth time. Bond stopped also, treading water softly. Cautiously he lifted his head and emptied water out of his goggles. By the time he looked again the ray had disappeared.

Bond had a Champion harpoon-gun with double rubbers.
The harpoon was tipped with a needle-sharp trident—a short-
range weapon, but the best for reef work. Bond pushed up the
safe and moved slowly forward, his fins pulsing softly just
below the surface so as to make no sound. He looked around
him, trying to pierce the misty horizons of the great hall of the
lagoon. He was looking for any big lurking shape. It would not
do to have a shark or a large barracuda as witness of the kill.
Fish sometimes scream when they are hurt, and even when
they do not the turbulence and blood caused by a sharp strug-
gle bring the scavengers. But there was not a living thing in
sight and the sand stretched away into the smoky wings like
the bare boards of a stage. Now Bond could see the faint out-
line on the bottom. He swam directly over it and lay motionless on the surface looking down. There was a tiny movement
in the sand. Two minute fountains of sand were dancing
above the nostril-like holes of the spiracles. Behind the holes
was the slight swelling of the thing's body. That was the target. An inch behind the holes. Bond estimated the possible
upward lash of the tail and slowly reached his gun down and
pulled the trigger.

Below him the sand erupted and for an anxious moment
Bond could see nothing. Then the harpoon line came taut and
the ray showed, pulling away from him while its tail, in reflex
aggression, lashed again and again over the body. At the base
of the tail Bond could see the jagged poison-spines standing
up from the trunk. These were the spines that were supposed
to have killed Ulysses, that Pliny said would destroy a tree. In
the Indian Ocean, where the sea poisons are at their most vir-
ulent, one scratch from the ray's sting would mean certain
death. Cautiously, keeping the ray on a taut line, Bond
trudged after the furiously wrestling fish. He swam to one side
to keep the line away from the lashing tail which could easily
sever it. This tail was the old slave-drivers' whip of the Indian

Ocean. Today it is illegal even to possess one in the Seychelles, but they are handed down in the families for use on faithless wives, and if the word goes round that this or that woman *a eu la crapule*, the Provençal name for the sting ray, it is as good as saying that that woman will not be about again for at least a week. Now the lashes of the tail were getting weaker and Bond swam round and ahead of the ray, pulling it after him towards the shore. In the shallows the ray went limp and Bond pulled it out of the water and well up on the beach. But he still kept away from it. It was as well he did so. Suddenly, at some move from Bond and perhaps in the hope of catching its enemy unawares, the giant ray leapt clean into the air. Bond sprang aside and the ray fell on its back and lay with its white underbelly to the sun and the great ugly sickle of the mouth sucking and panting.

Bond stood and looked at the sting-ray and wondered what to do next.

A short, fat white man in khaki shirt and trousers came out from under the palm trees and walked towards Bond through the scattering of sea-grape and sun-dried wrack above high-water mark. When he was near enough he called out in a laughing voice: 'The Old Man and the Sea! Who caught who?'

Bond turned. 'It *would* be the only man on the island who doesn't carry a machete. Fidele, be a good chap and call one of your men. This animal won't die, and he's got my spear stuck in him.'

Fidele Barbey, the youngest of the innumerable Barbeys who own nearly everything in the Seychelles, came up and stood looking down at the ray. 'That's a good one. Lucky you hit the right spot or he'd have towed you over the reef and you'd have had to let go your gun. They take the hell of a time to die. But come on. I've got to get you back to Victoria. Something's come up. Something good. I'll send one of your men for the gun. Do you want the tail?'

Bond smiled. 'I haven't got a wife. But what about some *raie au beurre noir* tonight?'

'Not tonight, my friend. Come. Where are your clothes?'

On their way down the coast road in the station wagon Fidele said: 'Ever hear of an American called Milton Krest? Well, apparently he owns the Krest hotels and a thing called the Krest Foundation. One thing I can tell you for sure. He owns the finest damned yacht in the Indian Ocean. Put in yesterday. The *Wavekrest*. Nearly two hundred tons. Hundred feet long. Everything in her from a beautiful wife down to a big transistor gramophone on gimbals so the waves won't jerk the needle. Wall-to-wall carpeting an inch deep. Air-conditioned throughout. The only dry cigarettes this side of the African continent, and the best after-breakfast bottle of champagne, since the last time I saw Paris.' Fidele Barbey laughed delightedly. 'My friend, that is one hell of a bloody fine ship, and if Mr Krest is a grand slam redoubled in bastards, who the hell cares?'

'Who cares anyway? What's it got to do with you—or me for the matter of that?'

'Just this, my friend. We are going to spend a few days sailing with Mr Krest—and Mrs Krest, the beautiful Mrs Krest. I have agreed to take the ship to Chagrin—the island I have spoken to you about. It is bloody miles from here—off the African Banks, and my family have never found any use for it except for collecting boobies' eggs. It's only about three feet above sea-level. I haven't been to the damned place for five years. Anyway, this man Krest wants to go there. He's collecting marine specimens, something to do with his Foundation, and there's some blasted little fish that's supposed to exist only around Chagrin Island. At least Krest says the only specimen in the world came from there.'

'Sounds rather fun. Where do I come in?'

'I knew you were bored and that you'd got a week before

you sail, so I said that you were the local underwater ace and that you'd soon find the fish if it was there, and anyway that I wouldn't go without you. Mr Krest was willing. And that's that. I knew you'd be fooling around somewhere down the coast, so I just drove along until one of the fishermen told me there was a crazy white man trying to commit suicide alone at Belle Anse and I knew that would be you.'

Bond laughed. 'Extraordinary the way these island people are afraid of the sea. You'd think they'd have got on terms with it by now. Damned few of the Seychellois can even swim.'

'Roman Catholic Church. Doesn't like them taking their clothes off. Bloody nonsense, but there it is. And as for being afraid, don't forget you've only been here for a month. Shark, barracuda—you just haven't met a hungry one. And stone-fish. Ever seen a man that's stepped on a stone-fish? His body bends backwards like a bow with the pain. Sometimes it's so frightful his eyes literally fall out of their sockets. They very seldom live.'

Bond said unsympathetically: 'They ought to wear shoes or bind their feet up when they go on the reef. They've got these fish in the Pacific and the giant clam into the bargain. It's damned silly. Everybody moans about how poor they are here, although the sea's absolutely paved with fish. And there are fifty varieties of cowrie under those rocks. They could make another good living selling those round the world.'

Fidele Barbey laughed boisterously. 'Bond for Governor! That's the ticket. Next meeting of LegCo I'll put the idea up. You're just the man for the job—far-sighted, full of ideas, plenty of drive. Cowries! That's splendid. They'll balance the budget for the first time since the patchouli boom after the War. "We sell sea-shells from the Seychelles." That'll be our slogan. I'll see you get the credit. You'll be Sir James in no time.'

'Make more money that way than trying to grow vanilla at a loss.' They continued to wrangle with light-hearted violence until the palm groves gave way to the giant sangdragon trees on the outskirts of the ramshackle capital of Mahe.

It had been nearly a month before when M had told Bond he was sending him to the Seychelles. 'Admiralty are having trouble with their new fleet base in the Maldives. Communists creeping in from Ceylon. Strikes, sabotage—the usual picture. May have to cut their losses and fall back on the Seychelles. A thousand miles farther south, but at least they look pretty secure. But they don't want to be caught again. Colonial Office say it's safe as houses. All the same I've agreed to send someone to give an independent view. When Makarios was locked up there a few years ago there were quite a few Security scares. Japanese fishing-boats hanging about, one or two refugee crooks from England, strong ties with France. Just go and have a good look.' M glanced out of the window at the driving March sleet. 'Don't get sunstroke.'

Bond's report, which concluded that the only conceivable security hazard in the Seychelles lay in the beauty and ready availability of the Seychelloises, had been finished a week before and then he had nothing to do but wait for the SS *Kampala* to take him to Mombasa. He was thoroughly sick of the heat and the drooping palm trees and the plaintive cry of the terns and the interminable conversations about copra. The prospect of a change delighted him.

Bond was spending his last week in the Barbey house, and after calling there to pick up their bags, they drove out to the end of Long Pier and left the car in the Customs shed. The gleaming white yacht lay half a mile out in the roadstead. They took a pirogue with an outboard motor across the glassy bay and through the opening in the reef. The *Wavekrest* was not beautiful—the breadth of beam and cluttered superstructure stunted her lines—but Bond could see at once that she was a real ship, built to cruise the world and not just the Florida Keys. She seemed deserted, but as they came alongside two smart-looking sailors in white shorts and singlets appeared and stood by the ladder with boat-hooks ready to fend the shabby pirogue off the yacht's gleaming paint. They took the two bags and one of them slid back an aluminium hatch and gestured for them to go down. A breath of what seemed to Bond to be almost freezing air struck him as he went through and down a few steps into the lounge.

The lounge was empty. It was not a cabin. It was a room of solid richness and comfort with nothing to associate it with the interior of a ship. The windows behind the half-closed venetian blinds were full size, as were the deep armchairs round the low central table. The carpet was the deepest pile in pale blue. The walls were panelled in a silvery wood and the ceiling was off-white. There was a desk with the usual writing-materials and a telephone. Next to the big gramophone was a sideboard laden with drinks. Above the sideboard was what looked like an extremely good Renoir—the head and shoulders of a pretty dark-haired girl in a black and white striped blouse. The impression of a luxurious living-room in a town house was completed by a large bowl of white and blue hyacinths on the central table and by the tidy range of magazines to one side of the desk.

'What did I tell you, James?'

Bond shook his head admiringly. 'This is certainly the way to treat the sea—as if it damned well didn't exist.' He breathed in deeply. 'What a relief to get a mouthful of fresh air. I'd almost forgotten what it tastes like.'

'It's the stuff outside that's fresh, feller. This is canned.' Mr Milton Krest had come quietly into the room and was standing looking at them. He was a tough, leathery man in his early fifties. He looked hard and fit, and the faded blue jeans, military-cut shirt and wide leather belt suggested that he made a fetish of doing so—looking tough. The pale brown eyes in the weather-beaten face were slightly hooded and their gaze was sleepy and contemptuous. The mouth had a downward twist that might be humorous or disdainful—probably the latter—and the words he had tossed into the room, innocuous in themselves except for the patronizing 'feller' had been tossed like small coin to a couple of coolies. To Bond the oddest thing about Mr Krest was his voice. It was a soft, most attractive lisping through the teeth. It was exactly the voice of the late Humphrey Bogart. Bond ran his eyes down the man from the sparse close-cropped black and grey hair, like iron filings sprinkled over the bullet head, to the tattooed eagle above a fouled anchor on the right forearm, and then down to the naked leathery feet that stood nautically square on the carpet. He thought: this man likes to be thought a Hemingway hero. I'm not going to get on with him.

Mr Krest came across the carpet and held out his hand. 'You Bond? Glad to have you aboard, sir.'

Bond was expecting the bone-crushing grip and parried it with stiffened muscles.

'Free-diving or aqualung?'

'Free, and I don't go deep. It's only a hobby.'

'Whadya do the rest of the time?'

'Civil Servant.'

Mr Krest gave a short barking laugh. 'Civility and Servitude. You English make the best goddam butlers and valets in the world. Civil Servant, you say? I reckon we're likely to get along fine. Civil Servants are just what I like to have around me.'

The click of the deck hatch sliding back saved Bond's temper. Mr Krest was swept from his mind as a naked sunburned girl came down the steps into the saloon. No, she wasn't quite naked after all, but the pale brown satin scraps of bikini were designed to make one think she was.

''Lo, treasure. Where have you been hiding? Long time no see. Meet Mr Barbey and Mr Bond, the fellers who are coming along.' Mr Krest raised a hand in the direction of the girl. 'Fellers, this is Mrs Krest. The fifth Mrs Krest. And just in case anybody should get any ideas, she loves Mr Krest. Don't you, treasure?'

'Oh don't be silly, Milt, you know I do.' Mrs Krest smiled prettily. 'How do you do, Mr Barbey. And Mr Bond. It's nice to have you with us. What about a drink?'

'Now just a minute, treas. Suppose you let me fix things aboard my own ship, hein?' Mr Krest's voice was soft and pleasant.

The woman blushed. 'Oh yes, Milt, of course.'

'Okay then, just so we know who's skipper aboard the good ship *Wavekrest*.' The amused smile embraced them all. 'Now then, Mr Barbey. What's your first name, by the way? Fidele, eh? That's quite a name. Old Faithful,' Mr Krest chuckled bonhomously. 'Well now, Fido how's about you and me go up on the bridge and get this little old skiff moving, hein? Mebbe you better take her out into the open sea and then you can set a course and hand over to Fritz. I'm the captain. He's the mate, and there are two for the engine-room and pantry. All three Germans. Only darned sailors left in Europe. And Mr Bond. First name? James, eh? Well, Jim what say you practise a bit of that civility and servitude on Mrs Krest. Call her Liz, by the way. Help her fix the canapés and so on for drinks before lunch. She was once a Limey too. You can swap yarns about Piccadilly Circus and the Dooks you both know. Okay? Move, Fido.' He sprang boyishly up the steps. 'Let's get the hell outa here.'

When the hatch closed, Bond let out a deep breath. Mrs Krest said apologetically: 'Please don't mind his jokes. It's just his sense of humour. And he's a bit contrary. He likes to see if he can rile people. It's very naughty of him. But it's really all in fun.'

Bond smiled reassuringly. How often did she have to make
this speech to people, try and calm the tempers of the people
Mr Krest had practised his 'sense of humour' on? He said: 'I
expect your husband needs a bit of knowing. Does he go on
the same way back in America?'

She said without bitterness: 'Only with me. He loves Americans. It's when he's abroad. You see, his father was a German, a Prussian really. He's got that silly German thing of
thinking Europeans and so on are decadent, that they aren't
any good any more. It's no use arguing with him. It's just a
thing he's got.'

So that was it! The old Hun again. Always at your feet or at
your throat. Sense of humour indeed! And what must this
woman have to put up with, this beautiful girl he had got hold
of to be his slave—his English slave? Bond said: 'How long
have you been married?'

'Two years. I was working as a receptionist in one of his
hotels. He owns the Krest Group, you know. It was wonderful. Like a fairy story. I still have to pinch myself sometimes
to make sure I'm not dreaming. This, for instance,' she
waved a hand at the luxurious room, 'and he's terribly good
to me. Always giving me presents. He's a very important
man in America, you know. It's fun being treated like royalty
wherever you go.'

'It must be. He likes that sort of thing, I suppose?'

'Oh yes.' There was resignation in the laugh. 'There's a lot
of the sultan in him. He gets quite impatient if he doesn't get
proper service. He says that when one's worked very hard to
get to the top of the tree one has a right to the best fruit that
grows there.' Mrs Krest found she was talking too freely. She
said quickly: 'But really, what am I saying? Anyone would
think we had known each other for years.' She smiled shyly.
'I suppose it's meeting someone from England. But I really
must go and get some more clothes on. I was sunbathing on

deck.' There came a deep rumble from below-deck amidships.
'There. We're off. Why don't you watch us leave harbour from
the afterdeck, and I'll come and join you in a minute. There's
so much I want to hear about London. This way.' She moved
past him and slid open a door. 'As a matter of fact, if you're
sensible, you'll stake a claim to this for the nights. There are
plenty of cushions, and the cabins are apt to get a bit stuffy in
spite of the air-conditioning.'

Bond thanked her, and walked out and shut the door behind
him. It was a big well-deck with hemp flooring and a cream-
coloured semicircular foam rubber settee in the stern. Rattan
chairs were scattered about and there was a serving-bar in one
corner. It crossed Bond's mind that Mr Krest might be a heavy
drinker. Was it his imagination, or was Mrs Krest terrified of
him? There was something painfully slavish in her attitude towards him. No doubt she had to pay heavily for her 'fairy
story'. Bond watched the green flanks of Mahe slowly slip
away astern. He guessed that their speed was about ten knots.
They would soon be at North Point and heading for the open
sea. Bond listened to the glutinous bubble of the exhaust and
idly thought about the beautiful Mrs Elizabeth Krest.

She could have been a model—probably had been before
she became a hotel receptionist—that respectable female calling that yet has a whiff of the high demi-monde about it—and
she still moved her beautiful body with the unselfconscious-
ness of someone who is used to going about with nothing, or
practically nothing, on. But there was none of the chill of the
model about her—it was a warm body and a friendly, confiding face. She might be thirty, certainly not more, and her pret-
tiness, for it was not more than that, was still immature. Her
best feature was the ash-blonde hair that hung heavily to the
base of her neck, but she seemed pleasantly lacking in vanity
about it. She didn't toss it about or fiddle with it, and it occurred to Bond that she didn't in fact show any signs of co-

quetry. She had stood quietly, almost docilely, with her large,
clear blue eyes fixed almost the whole time on her husband.
There was no lipstick on her mouth and no lacquer on her fingernails or toenails, and her eyebrows were natural. Did Mr
Krest perhaps order that it should be so—that she should be a
Germanic child of nature? Probably. Bond shrugged his
shoulders. They were certainly a curiously assorted couple—
the middle-aged Hemingway with the Bogart voice and the
pretty, artless girl. And there was tension in the air—in the
way she had cringed as he brought her to heel when she had
offered them drinks, in the forced maleness of the man. Bond
toyed idly with the notion that the man was impotent and that
all the tough, rude act was nothing more than exaggerated
virility-play. It certainly wasn't going to be easy to live with
for four or five days. Bond watched the beautiful Silhouette Island slip away to starboard and made a vow not to lose his
temper. What was that American expression? 'Eating crow'. It
would be an interesting mental exercise for him. He would eat
crow for five days and not let this damnable man interfere
with what should be a good trip.

'Well, feller. Taking it easy?' Mr Krest was standing on the
boat-deck looking down into the well. 'What have you done
with that woman I live with? Left her to do all the work, I
guess. Well, and why not? That's what they're for, ain't it?
Care to look over the ship? Fido's doin' a spell at the wheel
and I've got time on my hands.' Without waiting for an answer, Mr Krest bent and lowered himself down into the well-
deck, dropping the last four feet.

'Mrs Krest's putting on some clothes. Yes, I'd like to see over
the ship.'

Mr Krest fixed Bond with his hard, disdainful stare. ''Kay.
Well now, facts first. It's built by the Bronson Shipbuilding
Corporation. I happen to own ninety per cent of the stock, so
I got what I wanted. Designed by Rosenblatts—the top naval

architects. Hundred feet long, twenty-one broad, and draws six. Two five-hundred-horsepower Superior diesels. Top speed, fourteen knots. Cruises two thousand five hundred miles at eight. Air-conditioned throughout. Carrier Corporation designed two special five-ton units. Carries enough frozen food and liquor for a month. All we need is fresh water for the baths and showers. Right? Now let's go up front and you can see the crew's quarters, and we'll work back. And one thing, Jim,' Mr Krest stamped on the deck. 'This is the floor, see? And the head's the can. And if I want someone to stop doing whatever they're doing I don't shout "belay" I shout "hold it". Get me, Jim?'

Bond nodded amiably. 'I've got no objection. She's your ship.'

'*It*'s my ship,' corrected Mr Krest. 'That's another bit of damned nonsense, making a hunk of steel and wood a female. Anyway, let's go. You don't need to mind your head. Everything's a six-foot-two clearance.'

Bond followed Mr Krest down the narrow passage that ran the length of the ship, and for half an hour made appropriate comments on what was certainly the finest and most luxuriously designed yacht he had ever seen. In every detail the margin was for extra comfort. Even the crew's bath and shower was full size, and the stainless steel galley, or kitchen as Mr Krest called it, was as big as the Krest stateroom. Mr Krest opened the door of the latter without knocking. Liz Krest was at the dressing-table. 'Why, treasure,' said Mr Krest in his soft voice, 'I reckoned you'd be out there fixing the drink tray. You've sure been one heck of a time dressing up. Puttin' on a little extra Ritz for Jim, eh?'

'I'm sorry, Milt. I was just coming. A zip got stuck.' The girl hurriedly picked up a compact and made for the door. She gave them both a nervous half-smile and went out.

'Vermont birch panelling, Corning glass lamps, Mexican

tuft rugs. That sailing-ship picture's a genuine Montague Dawson, by the way . . .' Mr Krest's catalogue ran smoothly on. But Bond was looking at something that hung down almost out of sight by the bedside table on what was obviously Mr Krest's side of the huge double bed. It was a thin whip about three feet long with a leather-thonged handle. It was the tail of a sting-ray.

Casually Bond walked over to the side of the bed and picked it up. He ran a finger down its spiny gristle. It hurt his finger even to do that. He said: 'Where did you pick that up? I was hunting one of these animals this morning.'

'Bahrein. The Arabs use them on their wives.' Mr Krest chuckled easily. 'Haven't had to use more than one stroke at a time on Liz so far. Wonderful results. We call it my "Corrector".'

Bond put the thing back. He looked hard at Mr Krest and said: 'Is that so? In the Seychelles, where the creoles are pretty tough, it's illegal even to own one of those, let alone use it.'

Mr Krest moved towards the door. He said indifferently: 'Feller, this ship happens to be United States territory. Let's go get ourselves something to drink.'

Mr Krest drank three double bullshots—vodka in iced consommé—before luncheon, and beer with the meal. The pale eyes darkened a little and acquired a watery glitter, but the sibilant voice remained soft and unemphatic as, with a complete monopoly of the conversation, he explained the object of the voyage. 'Ya see, fellers, it's like this. In the States we have this Foundation system for the lucky guys that got plenty dough and don't happen to want to pay it into Uncle Sam's Treasury. You make a Foundation—like this one, the Krest Foundation—for charitable purposes—charitable to anyone, to kids, sick folk, the cause of science—you just give the money away to anyone or anything except yourself or your dependants and you escape tax on it. So I put a matter of ten million dollars into the Krest Foundation, and since I happen to like yachting and seeing the world I built this yacht with two million of the money and told the Smithsonian—that's our big natural history institution—that I would go to any part of the world and collect specimens for them. So that makes me a scientific expedition, see? For three months of every year I have a fine holiday that costs me just sweet Fatty Arbuckle!' Mr Krest looked to his guests for applause. 'Get me?'

Fidele Barbey shook his head doubtfully. 'That sounds fine, Mr Krest. But these rare specimens. They are easy to find? The Smithsonian it wants a giant panda, a sea-shell. You can get hold of these things where they have failed?'

Mr Krest slowly shook his head. He said sorrowfully: 'Feller, you sure were born yesterday. Money, that's all it takes. You want a panda? You buy it from some goddam zoo that can't afford central heating for its reptile house or wants to build a new block for its tigers or something. The sea-shell? You find a man that's got one and you offer him so much goddam money that even if he cries for a week he sells it to you. Sometimes you have a little trouble with Governments. Some goddam animal is protected or something. All right. Give you an example. I arrive at your island yesterday. I want a black parrot from Praslin Island. I want a giant tortoise from Aldabra. I want the complete range of your local cowries and I want this fish we're after. The first two are protected by law. Last evening I pay a call on your Governor after making certain inquiries in the town. Excellency, I says, I understand you want to build a public swimming-pool to teach the local kids to swim. Okay. The Krest Foundation will put up the money. How much? Five thousand, ten thousand? Okay, so it's ten thousand. Here's my cheque. And I write it out there and then. Just one little thing, Excellency, I says, holding on to the cheque. It happens I want a specimen of this black parrot you have here and one of these Aldabra tortoises. I understand they're protected by law. Mind if I take one of each back to

America for the Smithsonian? Well, there's a bit of a palaver, but seeing it's the Smithsonian and seeing I've still got hold of the cheque, in the end we shake hands on the deal and everyone's happy. Right? Well, on the way back I stop in the town to arrange with your nice Mr Abendana, the merchant feller, to have the parrot and tortoise collected and held for me, and I get talking about the cowries. Well, it so happens that this Mr Abendana has been collecting the dam' things since he was a child. He shows them to me. Beautifully kept—each one in its bit of cotton wool. Fine condition and several of those Isabella and Mappa ones I was asked particularly to watch out for. Sorry, he couldn't think of selling. They meant so much to him and so on. Crap! I just look at Mr Abendana and I say, how much? No no. He couldn't think of it. Crap again! I take out my chequebook and write a cheque for five thousand dollars and push it under his nose. He looks at it. Five thousand dollars! He can't stand it. He folds the cheque and puts it in his pocket and then the dam' sissy breaks down and weeps! Would you believe it?' Mr Krest opened his palms in disbelief. 'Over a few goddam sea-shells. So I just tell him to take it easy, and I pick up the trays of sea-shells and get the hell out of there before the crazy so-and-so shoots himself from remorse.'

Mr Krest sat back, well pleased with himself. 'Well, what d'you say to that, fellers? Twenty-four hours in the island and I've already knocked off three-quarters of my list. Pretty smart, eh, Jim?'

Bond said: 'You'll probably get a medal when you get home. What about this fish?'

Mr Krest got up from the table and rummaged in a drawer of his desk. He brought back a typewritten sheet. 'Here you are.' He read out: ' "Hildebrand Rarity. Caught by Professor Hildebrand of the University of the Witwatersrand in a net off Chagrin Island in the Seychelles group, April 1925".' Mr Krest looked up. 'And then there's a lot of scientific crap. I got them to put it into plain English, and here's the translation.' He turned back to the paper. '"This appears to be a unique member of the squirrel-fish family. The only specimen known, named the 'Hildebrand Rarity' after its discoverer, is six inches long. The colour is a bright pink with black transverse stripes. The anal, ventral and dorsal fins are pink. The tail fin is black. Eyes, large and dark blue. If found, care should be taken in handling this fish because all fins are even more sharply spiked than is usual with the rest of this family. Professor Hildebrand records that he found the specimen in three feet of water on the edge of the south-western reef".' Mr Krest threw the paper down on the table. 'Well, there you are, fellers. We're travelling about a thousand miles at a cost of several thousand dollars to try and find a goddam six-inch fish. And two years ago the Revenue people had the gall to suggest that my Foundation was a phoney!'

Liz Krest broke in eagerly: 'But that's just it, Milt, isn't it? It's really rather important to bring back plenty of specimens and things this time. Weren't those horrible tax people talking about disallowing the yacht and the expenses and so on for the last five years if we didn't show an outstanding scientific achievement? Wasn't that the way they put it?'

'Treasure,' Mr Krest's voice was soft as velvet. 'Just supposin' you keep that flippin' trap shut about my personal affairs. Yes?' The voice was amiable, nonchalant. 'You know what you just done, treas? You just earned yourself a little meeting with the Corrector this evening. That's what you've gone and done.'

The girl's hand flew to her mouth. Her eyes were wide. She said in a whisper: 'Oh no, Milt. Oh no, please.'

On the second day out, at dawn, they came up with Chagrin Island. It was first picked up by the radar—a small bump in the dead level line on the scanner—and then a minute blur on the great curved horizon grew with infinite slowness into half a mile of green fringed with white. It was extraordinary to come upon land after two days in which the yacht had seemed to be the only moving, the only living thing in an empty world. Bond had never seen or even clearly imagined the doldrums before. Now he realized what a terrible hazard they must have been in the days of sail—the sea of glass under a brazen sun, the foul, heavy air, the trail of small clouds along the rim of the world that never came closer, never brought wind or blessed rain. How must centuries of mariners have blessed this tiny dot in the Indian Ocean as they bent to the oars that moved the heavy ship perhaps a mile a day! Bond stood in the bows and watched the flying-fish squirt from beneath the hull as the blue-black of the sea slowly mottled into the brown and white and green of deep shoal. How wonderful that he would soon be walking and swimming again instead of just sitting and lying down. How wonderful to have a few hours' solitude—a few hours away from Mr Milton Krest!

They anchored outside the reef in ten fathoms and Fidele Barbey took them through the opening in the speedboat. In every detail Chagrin was the prototype coral island. It was about twenty acres of sand and dead coral and low scrub surrounded, after fifty yards of shallow lagoon, by a necklace of reef on which the quiet, long swell broke with a soft hiss. Clouds of birds rose when they landed—terns, boobies, men-of-war, frigates—but quickly settled again. There was a strong ammoniac smell of guano, and the scrub was white with it. The only other living things were the land-crabs that scuttled and scraped among the *liane sans fin* and the fiddler-crabs that lived in the sand.

The glare from the white sand was dazzling and there was no shade. Mr Krest ordered a tent to be erected and sat in it smoking a cigar while gear of various kinds was ferried

ashore. Mrs Krest swam and picked up seashells while Bond
and Fidele Barbey put on masks and, swimming in opposite
directions, began systematically to comb the reef all the way
round the island.

When you are looking for one particular species underwater—shell or fish or seaweed or coral formation—you have
to keep your brain and your eyes focused for that one indi-
vidual pattern. The riot of colour and movement and the endless variety of light and shadow fight your concentration all
the time. Bond trudged slowly along through the wonderland
with only one picture in his mind—a six-inch pink fish with
black stripes and big eyes—the second such fish man had
ever seen. 'If you see it,' Mr Krest had enjoined, 'just you let
out a yell and stay with it. I'll do the rest. I got a little something in the tent that's just the dandiest thing for catching fish
you ever saw.'

Bond paused to rest his eyes. The water was so buoyant that
he could lie face downwards on the surface without moving.
Idly he broke up a sea-egg with the tip of his spear and
watched the horde of glittering reef-fish darting for the shreds
of yellow flesh among the needle-sharp black spine. How in-
fernal that if he did find the Rarity it would benefit only Mr
Krest! Should he say nothing if he found it? Rather childish,
and anyway he was under contract, so to speak. Bond moved
slowly on, his eyes automatically taking up the search again
while his mind turned to considering the girl. She had spent
the previous day in bed. Mr Krest had said it was a headache.
Would she one day turn on him? Would she get herself a knife
or a gun and one night, when he reached for that damnable
whip, would she kill him? No. She was too soft, too malleable.
Mr Krest had chosen well. She was the stuff of slaves. And the
trappings of her 'fairytale' were too precious. Didn't she real-
ize that a jury would certainly acquit her if the sting-ray whip
was produced in court? She could have the trappings without

this dreadful, damnable man. Should Bond tell her that? Don't be ridiculous! How could he put it? 'Oh Liz, if you want to murder your husband, it'll be quite all right.' Bond smiled inside his mask. To hell with it! Don't interfere with other people's lives. She probably likes it—masochist. But Bond knew that that was too easy an answer. This was a girl who lived in fear. Perhaps she also lived in loathing. One couldn't read much in those soft blue eyes, but the windows had opened once or twice and a flash of something like a childish hate had shown through. Had it been hate? It had probably been indigestion. Bond put the Krests out of his mind and looked up to see how far round the island he had got. Fidele Barbey's snorkel was only a hundred yards away. They had nearly completed the circuit.

They came up with each other and swam to the shore and lay on the hot sand. Fidele Barbey said: 'Nothing on my side of the property except every fish in the world bar one. But I've had a stroke of luck. Ran into a big colony of green snail. That's the pearl shell as big as a small football. Worth quite a lot of money. I'll send one of my boats after them one of these days. Saw a blue parrot-fish that must have been a good thirty pounds. Tame as a dog, like all the fish round here. Hadn't got the heart to kill it. And if I had, there might have been trouble. Saw two or three leopard sharks cruising around over the reef. Blood in the water might have brought them through. Now I'm ready for a drink and something to eat. After that we can swap sides and have another go.'

They got up and walked along the beach to the tent. Mr Krest heard their voices and came out to meet them. 'No dice, eh?' He scratched angrily at an armpit. 'Goddam sandfly bit me. This is one hell of a godawful island. Liz couldn't stand the smell. Gone back to the ship. Guess we'd better give it one more going-over and then get the hell out of here. Help yourselves to some chow and you'll find cold beer in the icepack.

Here, gimme one of those masks. How do you use the dam' things? I guess I might as well take a peek at the sea's bottom while I'm about it.'

They sat in the hot tent and ate the chicken salad and drank beer, and moodily watched Mr Krest poking and peering about in the shallows. Fidele Barbey said: 'He's right, of course. These little islands are bloody awful places. Nothing but crabs and bird dung surrounded by too dam' much sea. It's only the poor bloody frozen Europeans that dream of coral islands. East of Suez, you won't find any sane man who gives a damn for them. My family owns about ten of them—decent-sized ones too, with small villages on them and a good income from copra and turtle. Well, you can have the whole bloody lot in exchange for a flat in Paris or London.'

Bond laughed. He began: 'Put an advertisement in *The Times* and you'd get sackloads . . .' when, fifty yards away, Mr Krest began to make frantic signals. Bond said: 'Either the bastard's found it or he's trodden on a guitar-fish,' and picked up his mask and ran down to the sea.

Mr Krest was standing up to his waist among the shallow beginnings of the reef. He jabbed his finger excitedly at the surface. Bond swam softly forward. A carpet of sea-grass ended in broken coral and an occasional niggerhead. A dozen varieties of butterfly and other reef-fish flirted among the rocks, and a small langouste quested towards Bond with its feelers. The head of a large green moray protruded from a hole, its half-open jaws showing the rows of needle teeth. Its golden eyes watched Bond carefully. Bond was amused to note that Mr Krest's hairy legs, magnified into pale tree-trunks by the glass, were not more than a foot away from the moray's jaws. He gave an encouraging poke at the moray with his spear, but the eel only snapped at the metal points and slid back out of sight. Bond stopped and floated, his eyes scanning the brilliant jungle. A red blur materialized through the far mist and came towards him. It circled closely beneath him as if showing itself off. The dark blue eyes examined him without fear. The small fish busied itself rather self-consciously with some algae on the underside of a niggerhead, made a dart at a speck of something suspended in the water, and then, as if leaving the stage after showing its paces, swam languidly off back into the mist.

Bond backed away from the moray's hole and put his feet to the ground. He took off his mask. He said to Mr Krest, who was standing gazing impatiently at him through his goggles: 'Yes, that's it all right. Better move quietly away from here. He won't go away unless he's frightened. These reef-fish stick pretty well to the same pastures.'

Mr Krest pulled off his mask. 'Goddam, I found it!' he said reverently. 'Well, goddam I did.' He slowly followed Bond to the shore.

Fidele Barbey was waiting for them. Mr Krest said boisterously: 'Fido, I found that goddam fish. Me—Milton Krest. Whadya know about that? After you two goddam experts had been at it all morning. I just took that mask of yours—first time I ever put one on, mark you—and I walked out and found the goddam fish in fifteen minutes flat. Whadya say to that eh, Fido?'

'That's good, Mr Krest. That's fine. Now how do we catch it?'

'Aha.' Mr Krest winked slowly. 'I got just the ticket for that. Got it from a chemist friend of mine. Stuff called Rotenone. Made from derris root. What the natives fish with in Brazil. Just pour it in the water, where it'll float over what you're after, and it'll get him as sure as eggs is eggs. Sort of poison. Constricts the blood vessels in their gills. Suffocates them. No effect on humans because no gills, see?' Mr Krest turned to Bond. 'Here, Jim. You go on out and keep watch. See the darned fish don't vamoose. Fido and I'll bring the stuff out there'—he pointed up-current from the vital area. 'I'll let go the Rotenone when you say the word. It'll drift down towards you. Right? But for lands sakes get the timing right. I've only got a five-gallon tin of this stuff. 'Kay?'

Bond said 'All right,' and walked slowly down and into the water. He swam lazily out to where he had stood before. Yes, everyone was still there, going about his business. The moray's pointed head was back again at the edge of its hole, the langouste again queried him. In a minute, as if it had a rendezvous with Bond, the Hildebrand Rarity appeared. This time it swam up quite close to his face. It looked through the glass at his eyes and then, as if disturbed by what it had seen there, darted out of range. It played around among the rocks for a while and then went off into a mist.

Slowly the little underwater world within Bond's vision began to take him for granted. A small octopus that had been camouflaged as a piece of coral revealed its presence and groped carefully down towards the sand. The blue and yellow langouste came a few steps out from under the rock, wondering about him. Some very small fish like minnows nibbled at his legs and toes, tickling. Bond broke a sea-egg for them and they darted to the better meal. Bond lifted his head. Mr Krest, holding the flat can, was twenty yards away to Bond's right. He would soon begin pouring, when Bond gave the sign, so that the liquid would get a good wide spread over the surface.

'Okay?' called Mr Krest.

Bond shook his head. 'I'll raise my thumb when he's back here. Then you'll have to pour fast.'

'Okay, Jim. You're at the bomb-sight.'

Bond put his head down. There was the little community, everyone busied with his affairs. Soon, to get one fish that someone vaguely wanted in a museum five thousand miles away, a hundred, perhaps a thousand small people were going to die. When Bond gave the signal, the shadow of death would come down on the stream. How long would the poison last? How far would it travel on down the reef? Perhaps it would not be thousands but tens of thousands that would die.

A small trunk-fish appeared, its tiny fins whirring like propellers. A rock beauty, gorgeous in gold and red and black, pecked at the sand, and a pair of the inevitable black and yellow striped sergeant-majors materialized from nowhere, attracted by the scent of the broken sea-egg.

Inside the reef, who was the predator in the world of small fishes? Who did they fear? Small barracuda? An occasional bill-fish? Now, a big, a fully grown predator, a man called Krest, was standing in the wings, waiting. And this one wasn't even hungry. He was just going to kill—almost for fun.

Two brown legs appeared in Bond's vision. He looked up. It was Fidele Barbey with a big creel strapped to his chest, and a long-handled landing-net.

Bond lifted his mask. 'I feel like the bomb-aimer at Nagasaki.'

'Fish are cold-blooded. They don't feel anything.'

'How do you know? I've heard them scream when they're hurt.'

Barbey said indifferently: 'They won't be able to scream with this stuff. It strangles them. What's eating you? They're only fish.'

'I know, I know.' Fidele Barbey had spent his life killing animals and fish. While he, Bond, had sometimes not hesitated to kill men. What was he fussing about? He hadn't minded killing the sting-ray. Yes, but that was an enemy fish. These down here were friendly people. People? The pathetic fallacy!

'Hey!' came the voice of Mr Krest. 'What's goin' on over there? This ain't no time for chewing the fat. Get that head down, Jim.'

Bond pulled down his mask and lay again on the surface. At once he saw the beautiful red shadow coming out of the far mists. The fish swam fast up to him as if it now took him for granted. It lay below him, looking up. Bond said into his mask: 'Get away from here, damn you.' He gave a sharp jab at the fish with his harpoon. The fish fled back into the mist. Bond lifted his head and angrily raised his thumb. It was a ridiculous and petty act of sabotage of which he was already ashamed. The dark brown oily liquid was pouring out on to the surface of the lagoon. There was time to stop Mr Krest before it was all gone—time to give him another chance at the Hildebrand Rarity. Bond stood and watched until the last drop was tilted out. To hell with Mr Krest!

Now the stuff was creeping slowly down on the current—a shiny, spreading stain which reflected the blue sky with a metallic glint. Mr Krest, the giant reaper, was wading down with it. 'Get set, fellers,' he called cheerfully. 'It's right up with you now.'

Bond put his head back under the surface. Everything was as before in the little community. And then, with stupefying suddenness, everyone went mad. It was as if they had all been seized with St Vitus's dance. Several fish looped the loop crazily and then fell like heavy leaves to the sand. The moray eel came slowly out of the hole in the coral, its jaws wide. It stood carefully upright on its tail and gently toppled sideways. The small langouste gave three kicks of its tail and turned over on its back, and the octopus let go its hold of the coral and drifted to the bottom upside-down. And then into the arena drifted the corpses from up-stream—white-bellied fish, shrimps, worms, hermit crabs, spotted and green morays, langoustes of all sizes. As if blown by some light breeze of death the clumsy bodies, their colours already fading, swept slowly past. A five-pound bill-fish struggled by with snapping beak, fighting death. Down-reef there were splashes on the surface as still bigger fish tried to make for safety. One by one, before Bond's eyes, the sea-urchins dropped off the rocks to make black ink-blots on the sand.

Bond felt a touch on his shoulder. Mr Krest's eyes were bloodshot with the sun and glare. He had put white sunburn paste on his lips. He shouted impatiently at Bond's mask, 'Where in hell's our goddam fish?'

Bond lifted his mask. 'Looks as if it managed to get away just before the stuff came down. I'm still watching for it.'

He didn't wait to hear Mr Krest's reply but got his head quickly under water again. Still more carnage, still more dead bodies. But surely the stuff had passed by now. Surely the area was safe just in case the fish, his fish because he had saved it, came back again! He stiffened. In the far mists there was a pink flash. It had gone. Now it was back again. Idly the Hildebrand Rarity swam towards him through the maze of channels between the broken outposts of the reef.

Not caring about Mr Krest, Bond raised his free hand out of the water and brought it down with a sharp slap. Still the fish came. Bond shifted the safe on his harpoon-gun and fired it in the direction of the fish. No effect. Bond put his feet down and began to walk towards the fish through the scattering of corpses. The beautiful red and black fish seemed to pause and quiver. Then it shot straight through the water towards Bond and dived down to the sand at his feet and lay still. Bond only had to bend to pick it up. There was not even a last flap from the tail. It just filled Bond's hand, lightly pricking the palm with the spiny black dorsal fin. Bond carried it back underwater so as to preserve its colours. When he got to Mr Krest he said 'Here,' and handed him the small fish. Then he swam away towards the shore.

That evening, with the *Wavekrest* heading for home down the path of a huge yellow moon, Mr Krest gave orders for what he called a 'wingding'. 'Gotta celebrate, Liz. This is terrific, a terrific day. Cleaned up the last target and we can get the hell out of these goddam Seychelles and get on back to civilization.

What say we make it to Mombasa when we've taken on board the tortoise and that goddam parrot? Fly to Nairobi and pick up a big plane for Rome, Venice, Paris—anywheres you care for. What say, treasure?' He squeezed her chin and cheeks in his big hand and made the pale lips pout. He kissed them drily. Bond watched the girl's eyes. They had shut tight. Mr Krest let go. The girl massaged her face. It was still white with his finger-marks.

'Gee, Milt,' she said half laughing, 'you nearly squashed me. You don't know your strength. But do let's celebrate. I think that would be lots of fun. And that Paris idea sounds grand. Let's do that, shall we? What shall I order for dinner?'

'Hell—caviare of course.' Mr Krest held his hands apart. 'One of those two-pound tins from Hammacher Schlemmer— the grade ten shot size, and all the trimmings. And that pink champagne.' He turned to Bond. 'That suit you, feller?'

'Sounds like a square meal.' Bond changed the subject. 'What have you done with the prize?'

'Formalin. Up on the boat-deck with some other jars of stuff we've picked up here and there—fish, shells. All safe in our home morgue. That's how we were told to keep the specimens. We'll airmail that damned fish when we get back to civilization. Give a Press conference first. Should make a big play in the papers back home. I've already radioed the Smithsonian and the news agencies. My accountants'll sure be glad of some Press cuttings to show those darned revenue boys.'

Mr Krest got very drunk that night. It did not show greatly. The soft Bogart voice became softer and slower. The round, hard head turned more deliberately on the shoulders. The lighter's flame took increasingly long to relight the cigar, and one glass was swept off the table. But it showed in the things Mr Krest said. There was a violent cruelty, a pathological desire to wound, quite near the surface in the man. That night, after dinner, the first target was James Bond. He was treated to

a soft-spoken explanation as to why Europe, with England
and France in the van, was a rapidly diminishing asset to the
world. Nowadays, said Mr Krest, there were only three powers—
America, Russia and China. That was the big poker game and
no other country had either the chips or the cards to come into
it. Occasionally some pleasant little country—and he admit-
ted they'd been pretty big league in the past—like England
would be lent some money so that they could take a hand
with the grown-ups. But that was just being polite like one
sometimes had to be—to a chum in one's club who'd gone
broke. No. England—nice people, mind you, good sports—
was a place to see the old buildings and the Queen and so on.
France? They only counted for good food and easy women.
Italy? Sunshine and spaghetti. Sanatorium, sort of. Germany?
Well, they still had some spunk, but two lost wars had
knocked the heart out of them. Mr Krest dismissed the rest of
the world with a few similar tags and then asked Bond for his
comments.

Bond was thoroughly tired of Mr Krest. He said he found Mr
Krest's point of view oversimplified—he might even say
naïve. He said: 'Your argument reminds me of a rather sharp
aphorism I once heard about America. Care to hear it?'

'Sure, sure.'

'It's to the effect that America has progressed from infancy to
senility without having passed through a period of maturity.'

Mr Krest looked thoughtfully at Bond. Finally he said:
'Why, say, Jim, that's pretty neat.' His eyes hooded slightly as
they turned towards his wife. 'Guess you'd kinda go along
with that remark of Jim's, eh, treasure? I recall you saying
once you reckoned there was something pretty childish about
the Americans. Remember?'

'Oh Milt.' Liz Krest's eyes were anxious. She had read the
signs. 'How can you bring that up? You know it was only
something casual I said about the comic sections of the pa-

pers. Of course I don't agree with what James says. Anyway, it was only a joke, wasn't it, James?'

'That's right,' said Bond. 'Like when Mr Krest said England had nothing but ruins and a queen.'

Mr Krest's eyes were still on the girl. He said softly: 'Shucks, treasure. Why are you looking so nervous? 'Course it was a joke.' He paused. 'And one I'll remember, treasure. One I'll sure remember.'

Bond estimated that by now Mr Krest had just about one whole bottle of various alcohols, mostly whisky, inside him. It looked to Bond as if, unless Mr Krest passed out, the time was not far off when Bond would have to hit Mr Krest just once very hard on the jaw. Fidele Barbey was now being given the treatment. 'These islands of yours, Fido. When I first looked them up on the map I thought it was just some specks of fly-dirt on the page.' Mr Krest chuckled. 'Even tried to brush them off with the back of my hand. Then I read a bit about them and it seemed to me my first thoughts had just about hit the nail on the head. Not much good for anything, are they, Fido? I wonder an intelligent guy like you doesn't get the hell out of there. Beachcombing ain't any kind of a life. Though I did hear one of your family had logged over a hundred illegitimate children. Mebbe that's the attraction, eh, feller?' Mr Krest grinned knowingly.

Fidele Barbey said equably: 'That's my uncle, Gaston. The rest of the family doesn't approve. It's made quite a hole in the family fortune.'

'Family fortune, eh?' Mr Krest winked at Bond. 'What's it in? Cowrie-shells?'

'Not exactly.' Fidele Barbey was not used to Mr Krest's brand of rudeness. He looked mildly embarrassed. 'Though we made quite a lot out of tortoiseshell and mother-of-pearl about a hundred years ago when there was a rage for these things. Copra's always been our main business.'

'Using the family bastards as labour, I guess. Good idea.
Wish I could fix something like that in my home circle.' He
looked across at his wife. The rubber lips turned still further
down. Before the next gibe could be uttered, Bond had pushed
his chair back and had gone out into the well-deck and pulled
the door shut behind him.

Ten minutes later, Bond heard feet coming softly down the
ladder from the boat-deck. He turned. It was Liz Krest. She
came over to where he was standing in the stern. She said in
a strained voice: 'I said I'd go to bed. But then I thought I'd
come back here and see if you'd got everything you want. I'm
not a very good hostess, I'm afraid. Are you sure you don't
mind sleeping out here?'

'I like it. I like this kind of air better than the canned stuff
inside. And it's rather wonderful to have all those stars to look
at. I've never seen so many before.'

She said eagerly, grasping at a friendly topic: 'I like Orion's
Belt and the Southern Cross the best. You know, when I was
young, I used to think the stars were really holes in the sky.
I thought the world was surrounded by a great big black sort
of envelope, and that outside it the universe was full of
bright light. The stars were just holes in the envelope that let
little sparks of light through. One gets terribly silly ideas
when one's young.' She looked up at him, wanting him not
to snub her.

Bond said: 'You're probably quite right. One shouldn't believe all the scientists say. They want to make everything dull.
Where did you live then?'

'At Ringwood in the New Forest. It was a good place to be
brought up. A good place for children. I'd like to go there
again one day.'

Bond said: 'You've certainly come a long way since then.
You'd probably find it pretty dull.'

She reached out and touched his sleeve. 'Please don't say

that. You don't understand—' there was an edge of despera-
tion in the soft voice—'I can't bear to go on missing what other
people have—ordinary people. I mean,' she laughed nerv-
ously, 'you won't believe me, but just to talk like this for a few
minutes, to have someone like you to talk to, is something I'd
almost forgotten.' She suddenly reached for his hand and held
it hard. 'I'm sorry. I just wanted to do that. Now I'll go to bed.'

The soft voice came from behind them. The speech had
slurred, but each word was carefully separated from the next.
'Well, well. Whadya know? Necking with the underwater
help!'

Mr Krest stood framed in the hatch to the saloon. He stood
with his legs apart and his arms upstretched to the lintel
above his head. With the light behind him he had the silhouette of a baboon. The cold, imprisoned breath of the saloon
rushed out past him and for a moment chilled the warm night
air in the well-deck. Mr Krest stepped out and softly pulled
the door to behind him.

Bond took a step towards him, his hands held loosely at his
sides. He measured the distance to Mr Krest's solar plexus. He
said: 'Don't jump to conclusions, Mr Krest. And watch your
tongue. You're lucky not to have got hurt so far tonight. Don't
press your luck. You're drunk. Go to bed.'

'Oho! Listen to the cheeky feller.' Mr Krest's moon-burned
face turned slowly from Bond to his wife. He made a contemptuous, Hapsburg-lip grimace. He took a silver whistle out
of his pocket and whirled it round on its string. 'He sure don't
get the picture, does he, treasure? You ain't told him that those
Heinies up front ain't just for ornament?' He turned back to
Bond. 'Feller, you move any closer and I blow this—just once.
And you know what? It'll be the old heave-ho for Mr goddam
Bond'—he made a gesture towards the sea—'over the side.
Man overboard. Too bad. We back up to make a search and
you know what, feller? Just by chance we back up into you

with those twin screws. Would you believe it! What lousy bad luck for that nice feller Jim we were all getting so fond of!' Mr Krest swayed on his feet. 'Dya get the photo, Jim? Okay, so let's all be friends again and get some shut-eye.' He reached for the lintel of the hatch and turned to his wife. He lifted his free hand and slowly crooked a finger. 'Move, treasure. Time for bed.'

'Yes, Milt.' The wide, frightened eyes turned sideways. 'Goodnight, James.' Without waiting for an answer, she ducked under Mr Krest's arm and almost ran through the saloon.

Mr Krest lifted a hand. 'Take it easy, feller. No hard feelings, eh?'

Bond said nothing. He went on looking hard at Mr Krest.

Mr Krest laughed uncertainly. He said: 'Okay then.' He stepped into the saloon and slid the door shut. Through the window Bond watched him walk unsteadily across the saloon and turn out the lights. He went into the corridor and there was a momentary gleam from the stateroom door, and then that too went dark.

Bond shrugged his shoulders. God, what a man! He leant against the stern rail and watched the stars and the flashes of phosphorescence in the creaming wake, and set about washing his mind clear and relaxing the coiled tensions in his body.

Half an hour later, after taking a shower in the crew's bathroom forrard, Bond was making a bed for himself among the piled Dunlopillo cushions when he heard a single, heart-rending scream. It tore briefly into the night and was smothered. It was the girl. Bond ran through the saloon and down the passage. With his hand on the stateroom door, he stopped. He could hear her sobs and, above them, the soft even drone of Mr Krest's voice. He took his hand away from the latch.

Hell! What was it to do with him? They were man and wife. If she was prepared to stand this sort of thing and not kill her husband, or leave him, it was no good Bond playing Sir Galahad. Bond walked slowly back down the passage. As he was crossing the saloon the scream, this time less piercing, rang out again. Bond cursed fluently and went out and lay down on his bed and tried to focus his mind on the soft thud of the diesels. How could a girl have so little guts? Or was it that women could take almost anything from a man? Anything except indifference? Bond's mind refused to unwind. Sleep got further and further away.

An hour later Bond had reached the edge of unconsciousness when, up above him on the boat-deck, Mr Krest began to snore. On the second night out from Port Victoria, Mr Krest had left his cabin in the middle of the night and had gone up to the hammock that was kept slung for him between the speedboat and the dinghy. But that night he had not snored. Now he was snoring with those deep, rattling, utterly lost snores that come from big blue sleeping-pills on top of too much alcohol.

This was too damned much. Bond looked at his watch. One-thirty. If the snoring didn't stop in ten minutes, Bond would go down to Fidele Barbey's cabin and sleep on the floor, even if he did wake up stiff and frozen in the morning.

Bond watched the gleaming minute-hand slowly creep round the dial. Now! He had got to his feet and was gathering up his shirt and shorts when, from up on the boat-deck, there came a heavy crash. The crash was immediately followed by scrabbling sounds and a dreadful choking and gurgling. Had Mr Krest fallen out of his hammock? Reluctantly Bond dropped his things back on the deck and walked over and climbed the ladder. As his eyes came level with the boat-deck, the choking stopped. Instead there was another, a more dread-

ful sound—the quick drumming of heels. Bond knew that
sound. He leapt up the last steps and ran towards the figure
lying spreadeagled on its back in the bright moonlight. He
stopped and knelt slowly down, aghast. The horror of the
strangled face was bad enough, but it was not Mr Krest's
tongue that protruded from his gaping mouth. It was the tail
of a fish. The colours were pink and black. It was the Hildebrand Rarity!

The man was dead—horribly dead. When the fish had been
crammed into his mouth, he must have reached up and desperately tried to tug it out. But the spines of the dorsal and
anal fins had caught inside the cheeks and some of the spiny
tips now protruded through the blood-flecked skin round the
obscene mouth. Bond shuddered. Death must have come inside a minute. But what a minute!

Bond slowly got to his feet. He walked over to the racks of
glass specimen jars and peered under the protective awning.
The plastic cover of the end jar lay on the deck beside it. Bond
wiped it carefully on the tarpaulin, and then, holding it by the
tips of his fingernails, laid it loosely back over the mouth of
the jar.

He went back and stood over the corpse. Which of the two
had done this? There was a touch of fiendish spite in using
the treasured prize as a weapon. That suggested the woman.
She certainly had her reasons. But Fidele Barbey, with his
creole blood, would have had the cruelty and at the same
time the macabre humour. *'Je lui ai foutu son sacré poisson
dans la gueule.'* Bond could hear him say the words. If, after
Bond had left the saloon, Mr Krest had needled the Seychellois just a little bit further—particularly about his family or
his beloved islands—Fidele Barbey would not have hit him
then and there, or used a knife, he would have waited and
plotted.

Bond looked round the deck. The snoring of the man could have been a signal for either of them. There were ladders to the boat-deck from both sides of the cabin-deck amidships. The man at the wheel in the pilot-house forrard would have heard nothing above the noise from the engine-room. To pick the small fish out of its formalin bath and slip it into Mr Krest's gaping mouth would have only needed seconds. Bond shrugged. Whichever had done it had not thought of the consequences—of the inevitable inquest, perhaps of a trial in which he, Bond, would be an additional suspect. They were certainly all going to be in one hell of a mess unless he could tidy things up.

Bond glanced over the edge of the boat-deck. Below was the three-foot-wide strip of deck that ran the length of the ship. Between this and the sea there was a two-foot-high rail. Supposing the hammock had broken, and Mr Krest had fallen and rolled under the speedboat and over the edge of the upper deck, could he have reached the sea? Hardly, in this dead calm but that was what he was going to have done.

Bond got moving. With a table-knife from the saloon, he carefully frayed and then broke one of the main cords of the hammock so that the hammock trailed realistically on the deck. Next, with a damp cloth, he cleaned up the specks of blood on the woodwork and the drops of formalin that led from the specimen jar. Then came the hardest part—handling the corpse. Carefully Bond pulled it to the very edge of the deck and himself went down the ladder and, bracing himself, reached up. The corpse came down on top of him in a heavy, drunken embrace. Bond staggered under it to the low rail and eased it over. There was a last hideous glimpse of the obscenely bulging face, a sickening fume of stale whisky, a heavy splash, and it was gone and rolling sluggishly away in the small waves of the wake. Bond flattened himself back against the saloon hatchway, ready to slip through if the helmsman came aft to investigate. But there was no movement forrard and the iron tramp of the diesels held steady.

Bond sighed deeply. It would be a very troublesome coroner who brought in anything but misadventure. He went back to the boat-deck, gave it a final look over, disposed of the knife and the wet cloth, and went down the ladder to his bed in the well. It was two-fifteen. Bond was asleep inside ten minutes.

By pushing the speed up to twelve knots they made North Point by six o'clock that evening. Behind them the sky was ablaze with red and gold streaked across aquamarine. The two men, with the woman between them, stood at the rail of the well-deck and watched the brilliant shore slip by across the mother-of-pearl mirror of the sea. Liz Krest was wearing a white linen frock with a black belt and a black and white handkerchief round her neck. The mourning colours went well with the golden skin. The three people stood stiffly and rather self-consciously, each one nursing his own piece of secret knowledge, each one anxious to convey to the other two that their particular secrets were safe with him.

That morning there had seemed to be a conspiracy among the three to sleep late. Even Bond had not been awakened by the sun until ten o'clock. He showered in the crew's quarters and chatted with the helmsman before going below to see what had happened to Fidele Barbey. He was still in bed. He said he had a hangover. Had he been very rude to Mr Krest? He couldn't remember much about it except that he seemed to recall Mr Krest being very rude to him. 'You remember what I said about him from the beginning, James? A grand slam redoubled in bastards. Now do you agree with me? One of these days someone's going to shut that soft ugly mouth of his for ever.'

Inconclusive. Bond had fixed himself some breakfast in the galley and was eating it there when Liz Krest had come in to do the same. She was dressed in a pale blue shantung kimono to her knees. There were dark rings under her eyes and she ate her breakfast standing. But she seemed perfectly calm and at ease. She whispered conspiratorially: 'I do apologize about last night. I suppose I'd had a bit too much to drink too. But do forgive Milt. He's really awfully nice. It's only when he's had a bit too much that he gets sort of difficult. He's always sorry the next morning. You'll see.'

When eleven o'clock came and neither of the other two showed any signs of, so to speak, blowing the gaff, Bond decided to force the pace. He looked very hard at Liz Krest who was lying on her stomach in the well-deck reading a magazine. He said: 'By the way where's your husband? Still sleeping it off?'

She frowned. 'I suppose so. He went up to his hammock on the boat-deck. I've no idea what time. I took a sleeping-pill and went straight off.'

Fidele Barbey had a line out for amberjack. Without looking round he said: 'He's probably in the pilot-house.'

Bond said: 'If he's still asleep on the boat-deck, he'll be getting the hell of a sunburn.'

Liz Krest said: 'Oh, poor Milt! I hadn't thought of that. I'll go and see.'

She climbed the ladder. When her head was above the level of the boat-deck she stopped. She called down, anxiously: 'Jim. He's not here. And the hammock's broken.'

Bond said: 'Fidele's probably right. I'll have a look forrard.'

He went to the pilot-house. Fritz, the mate and the engineer were there. Bond said: 'Anyone seen Mr Krest?'

Fritz looked puzzled. 'No, sir. Why? Is anything wrong?'

Bond flooded his face with anxiety. 'He's not aft. Here, come on! Look round everywhere. He was sleeping on the boat-deck. He's not there and his hammock's broken. He was rather the worse for wear last night. Come on! Get cracking!'

When the inevitable conclusion had been reached, Liz Krest had a short but credible fit of hysterics. Bond took her to her cabin and left her there in tears. 'It's all right, Liz,' he said. 'You stay out of this. I'll look after everything. We'll have to radio Port Victoria and so on. I'll tell Fritz to put on speed. I'm afraid it's hopeless turning back to look. There've been six hours of daylight when he couldn't have fallen overboard without being heard or seen. It must have been in the night. I'm afraid anything like six hours in these seas is just not on.'

She stared at him, her eyes wide. 'You mean—you mean sharks and things?'

Bond nodded.

'Oh Milt! Poor darling Milt! Oh, why did this have to happen?'

Bond went out and softly shut the door.

The yacht rounded Cannon Point and reduced speed. Keeping well away from the broken reef, it slid quietly across the broad bay, now lemon and gunmetal in the last light, towards the anchorage. The small township beneath the mountains was already dark with indigo shadow in which a sprinkling of yellow lights showed. Bond saw the Customs and Immigration launch move off from Long Pier to meet them. The little community would already be buzzing with the news that would have quickly leaked from the radio station to the Seychelles Club and then, through the members' chauffeurs and staffs, into the town.

Liz Krest turned to him. 'I'm beginning to get nervous. Will you help me through the rest of this—these awful formalities and things?'

'Of course.'

Fidele Barbey said: 'Don't worry too much. All these people are my friends. And the Chief Justice is my uncle. We shall all have to make a statement They'll probably have the inquest tomorrow. You'll be able to leave the day after.'

'You really think so?' A dew of sweat had sprung below her eyes. 'The trouble is, I don't really know where to leave for, or what to do next. I suppose,' she hesitated, not looking at Bond. 'I suppose, James, you wouldn't like to come on to Mombasa? I mean, you're going there, anyway, and I'd be able to get you there a day earlier than this ship of yours, this Camp something.'

'*Kampala*.' Bond lit a cigarette to cover his hesitation. Four days in a beautiful yacht with this girl! But the tail of that fish sticking out of the mouth! Had she done it? Or had Fidele, who would know that his uncles and cousins on Mahe would somehow see that he came to no harm? If only one of them would make a slip. Bond said easily: 'That's terribly nice of you, Liz. Of course I'd love to come.'

Fidele Barbey chuckled. 'Bravo, my friend. And I would love to be in your shoes, but for one thing. That damned fish. It is a great responsibility. I like to think of you both being deluged with cables from the Smithsonian about it. Don't forget that you are now both trustees of a scientific Koh-i-noor. And you know what these Americans are. They'll worry the life out of you until they've got their hands on it.'

Bond's eyes were hard as flint as he watched the girl. Surely that put the finger on her. Now he would make some excuse— get out of the trip. There had been something about that particular way of killing a man . . .

But the beautiful, candid eyes did not flicker. She looked up into Fidele Barbey's face and said, easily, charmingly: 'That won't be a problem. I've decided to give it to the British Museum.'

James Bond noticed that the sweat dew had now gathered at her temples. But, after all, it was a desperately hot evening . . .

The thud of the engines stopped and the anchor chain roared down into the quiet bay.

FOR THE BEST IN PAPERBACKS, LOOK FOR THE Ⓟ

In every corner of the world, on every subject under the sun, Penguin represents quality and variety—the very best in publishing today.

For complete information about books available from Penguin—including Penguin Classics, Penguin Compass, and Puffins—and how to order them, write to us at the appropriate address below. Please note that for copyright reasons the selection of books varies from country to country.

In the United States: Please write to *Penguin Group (USA), P.O. Box 12289 Dept. B, Newark, New Jersey 07101-5289* or call 1-800-788-6262.

In the United Kingdom: Please write to *Dept. EP, Penguin Books Ltd, Bath Road, Harmondsworth, West Drayton, Middlesex UB7 0DA.*

In Canada: Please write to *Penguin Books Canada Ltd, 10 Alcorn Avenue, Suite 300, Toronto, Ontario M4V 3B2.*

In Australia: Please write to *Penguin Books Australia Ltd, P.O. Box 257, Ringwood, Victoria 3134.*

In New Zealand: Please write to *Penguin Books (NZ) Ltd, Private Bag 102902, North Shore Mail Centre, Auckland 10.*

In India: Please write to *Penguin Books India Pvt Ltd, 11 Panchsheel Shopping Centre, Panchsheel Park, New Delhi 110 017.*

In the Netherlands: Please write to *Penguin Books Netherlands bv, Postbus 3507, NL-1001 AH Amsterdam.*

In Germany: Please write to *Penguin Books Deutschland GmbH, Metzlerstrasse 26, 60594 Frankfurt am Main.*

In Spain: Please write to *Penguin Books S. A., Bravo Murillo 19, 1° B, 28015 Madrid.*

In Italy: Please write to *Penguin Italia s.r.l., Via Benedetto Croce 2, 20094 Corsico, Milano.*

In France: Please write to *Penguin France, Le Carré Wilson, 62 rue Benjamin Baillaud, 31500 Toulouse.*

In Japan: Please write to *Penguin Books Japan Ltd, Kaneko Building, 2-3-25 Koraku, Bunkyo-Ku, Tokyo 112.*

In South Africa: Please write to *Penguin Books South Africa (Pty) Ltd, Private Bag X14, Parkview, 2122 Johannesburg.*